A Tapestry of Colours 1
Stories from Asia

Edited by
Anitha Devi Pillai

Marshall Cavendish
Editions

Reprinted 2022

Published by Marshall Cavendish Editions
An imprint of Marshall Cavendish International

A member of the
Times Publishing Group

Other Marshall Cavendish Offices:
Marshall Cavendish Corporation, 800 Westchester Ave, Suite N-641, Rye Brook,
NY 10573, USA • Marshall Cavendish International (Thailand) Co Ltd, 253 Asoke,
16th Floor, Sukhumvit 21 Road, Klongtoey Nua, Wattana, Bangkok 10110, Thailand
• Marshall Cavendish (Malaysia) Sdn Bhd, Times Subang, Lot 46, Subang Hi-Tech
Industrial Park, Batu Tiga, 40000 Shah Alam, Selangor Darul Ehsan, Malaysia

Marshall Cavendish is a registered trademark of Times Publishing Limited

National Library Board, Singapore Cataloguing in Publication Data

Title: A tapestry of colours. 2 : stories from Asia / Edited by Anitha Devi Pillai.
Description: Singapore : Marshall Cavendish Editions, [2021]
Identifiers: OCN 1247399953 | ISBN 978-981-4928-73-1
Subjects: LCSH: Short stories, English—Asia. | Short stories, Singaporean (English)
Classification: DDC 823.0108—dc23

Printed in Singapore

Cover image: Shutterstock, by Marukopum

Contents

Foreword

The two-volume set of *A Tapestry of Colours – Stories from Asia*, edited by Dr Anitha Devi Pillai, offers teachers a uniquely valuable resource for classrooms and an extraordinary opportunity to help students discover for themselves what the reading of literature can offer to them in delight and in their expanded understanding of human experience. Of all the literary genres, the genre of the short story seems to me most suitable for classroom use. Short stories are, by definition, fiction that can be read in what used to be called "one sitting." I love the idea of a "sitting," and recently saw it defined as 20 minutes to an hour. In my own years as an elementary and secondary student, 20 minutes may have been the outer limit of my capacity to sit in one place. But a good story might hold me somewhat longer, and the stories in this volume promise to hold students long enough to be read, if not always in one sitting, surely in no more than two sittings and usually well within the time typically allotted in a classroom both for reading and for discussion of what was read.

The individual stories in these two volumes, moreover, are presented in a textual setting that is likely to promote and deepen the reflection and discussion that inevitably follows classroom reading – and certainly ought to follow reading, if students are to gain the full benefit from what they have read. The setting I am referring to for these stories is the apparatus provided in these volumes for every included story, whereby each story is prefaced by a short personal note from its writer about the cultural context in which the story was written, and followed by the writer's account of how the completed story came into being: what occasioned it, what problems it presented, what the writer was hoping to accomplish for the reader and so on. The effect of this framing material is, first, to enhance a reader's interest in the story, based on the reader's intensified sense of personal involvement with the writer, and second, to deepen a reader's understanding of the story, by ensuring that the reader understands the cultural references or historical moment, or personal circumstances that are the context for each individual story and writer.

We must remember that short stories are not specialized technical kinds of discourse (though they can take on new and unfamiliar forms and include entirely original features), but they represent the literary genre that is most natural to all human beings in every human society. They have their anthropological origins in dreams and gossip and myths and family adventures and personal experiences that are told in everyday life and are frequently worth re-telling. Every child and adult knows from living with other human beings how to listen to and respond to such stories. As teachers of literary short stories, we must build on rather than cancel out the competence of all our students as persons with extensive experience in hearing and enjoying stories.

And, given the excellent collection of stories presented here, with their illuminating introductions and intimate accounts of their generative occasions, almost no student will be able to resist the essential dimension of literary experience – that of becoming immersed in the story itself and thereby ready for rich conversation about what happened and why we care.

Sheridan Blau, PhD
Professor of Practice in the Teaching of English
Department of Arts and Humanities
Teachers College, Columbia University;
Emeritus Professor of English and Education
University of California, Santa Barbara

Preface

The short story is a very welcoming text type as its brevity and accessibility make it an excellent platform to explore unknown topics and difficult subjects. It also gives readers an insight into other worlds and lives of people across the world within a short period of time.

In fact, short story readers were found to be more thoughtful, creative and willing to consider competing viewpoints than non-fictional essay readers by Maja Djikic, Keith Oatley and Mihnea Moldoveanu from the University of Toronto. Short story readers were also found to be open to exploring unfamiliar territories which helped to broaden their minds and engage them in honest conversations about the lives and actions of others. In other words, short stories have been found to be effective in nurturing empathetic readers who are respectful of other cultures. As the prolific author Neil Gaiman once said, "Fiction gives us empathy: it puts us inside the minds of other people, gives us the gifts of seeing the world through their eyes."

These two collections of short stories, *A Tapestry of Colours 1 & 2 – Stories from Asia*, aim to do just that by presenting stories from our neighbours in Asia and providing us with a means to understand them through narratives. This makes these collections of stories a valuable resource in the language and literature classroom as well.

Emeritus Professor Sheridan Blau, a well-renowned academic of English and Education at Teacher's College, Columbia University, illuminates the unique nature of these two books, which connects each short story to its setting and the writer and the importance of doing so. I am deeply grateful that Professor

Blau's insightful comments captured the essence of the value of short stories to readers.

The contributing writers have captured the spirit and multiple facets of living and growing up in various parts of Asia (Singapore, Malaysia, Thailand, Philippines, Indonesia, China, Korea, Japan, Bangladesh and India). The writers have to be commended for their collective willingness to share notes on their craft as they add an important perspective. I am indebted to the writers for their support and am deeply grateful to them for helping to create a meaningful conversation about the different facets of Asia.

I am also grateful to the following educators and passionate fiction lovers who have helped to provide comments on the short stories to make them very relatable and meaningful for youths: Aileen Chai, Amanda Sarah Chin, Amala Rajan, Azeena Badarudeen, Bernice Xu, Geetha Creffield, John Praveen Raj, Dr Mary Ellis, Michelle Wong, Priyanka Chakraborty, Selvarani Suppiah, Shafiq Rafi, Shalini Damodaran and Tivona Low. Special thanks to Sumi Baby Thomas, the research assistant on this project.

Last but not least, I would like to thank the publishing team from Marshall Cavendish International: Melvin Neo, Mindy Pang and Anita Teo for bringing this set of books to life and to the public.

Anitha Devi Pillai

Voices

Anitha Devi Pillai

Some say writers are born talented and destined for great success from the start. Others say that if one is an avid reader, then one learns about what constitutes good text. It comes from the age-old belief that good writers are devoted students of the craft and hence read voraciously and indiscriminately. Yet, many avid readers do not become writers. Instead, they are content to sit amongst books in their favourite bookstore, library or the comforts of home marvelling over the worlds they read about and often escaping into these worlds.

I believe that writers are born in the writing classroom where they discover themselves and the power of crafting a narrative for an audience. The first moment when one discovers that one is able to tell a story convincingly and able to keep an audience captive is magical. Their teachers are their first mentors and sometimes the only readers of the many attempts of these budding writers. It goes without saying that the writing teacher is a nurturing ally or a formidable (and cruel) adversary in a writer's journey.

13-year-old Sudiksha Menon

I placed my neatly written composition in a plastic folder before putting it into my schoolbag. I had been tasked to write a letter as a writing assignment in my English Language class. I had written a letter to my grandaunt who lived in India and whom I had met for the first time in my life over the school vacation in December, two months ago. I could tell that my grandaunt was really fond of her elder brother, my grandfather. The siblings had both cried when they met, and again when they had to say goodbye. They had not seen each other in more than 15 years!

Later, my mother told me that my grandaunt had left Singapore at the age of 20 in the 1970s, after she had married an engineer from our ancestral home town, Kollam in Kerala. I wondered if she had known then that she would never return or see her land of birth ever again.

So when I was tasked to write a letter by Ms Seah, my secondary one English teacher, I decided to write to my grandaunt and invite her to visit Singapore for my grandfather's surprise 70th birthday celebration. I even printed a photograph of my grandaunt and my family that we had taken together in India during my vacation and attached it to the letter. Thankfully, my grandaunt had just sent the photograph along with several others via WhatsApp a few days ago. That came in handy.

I was certain that my composition would stand out. It was neatly written, carefully proofread and even included a photograph. The extra touch of pasting a printout of the photograph to the letter somehow made the composition more real – like a real invitation. I had seen my mother attach photographs to emails. I could not wait to see Ms Seah's expression when she saw my composition and the extra touch that I had put in. Once Ms Seah noticed me, I would make the announcement.

This was the day I would tell her that I was going to be a successful writer when I grew up.

9-year-old Sudiksha Menon

I stared at the mango-leaf green popsicle in my hand. It was beginning to drip down my fingers to my elbow. I hoped it wouldn't melt away too quickly before I reached my flat. My mother had to be home by this time.

"Please don't melt … please don't melt," I chanted all the way back to my apartment in Jurong West, lugging my heavy schoolbag on my tiny shoulders.

My mother was exactly where I thought she would be. She was seated at her table in the study, bent over her notes, with a red pen in her hands. You see, my mother was a secondary school English teacher at Banyan Secondary and it was her usual routine to start grading papers as soon as she got home.

"For you ... I made it in class today," I said as I gingerly handed over the melting popsicle to her.

If my mother was amused by the colour of the popsicle, she didn't show it. I watched the tip of the popsicle disappear into her mouth. My mother exaggerated every move. She had to be pleased that I had saved the treat that I made in school for her.

But the next second, she grimaced. I wasn't sure if it was the ice or the taste. After a few seconds, my mother took a deep breath, and quickly polished off the rest of the popsicle.

"How did you make this, Sudiksha?"

I didn't know if I should tell my mother that I had taken her daily breakfast of bitter gourd and ginger juice to school that day to make this popsicle. It wasn't my fault that my mother was on yet another diet. This time, she was on a no-sugar diet. So there were no fruit juices or soft drinks. There were no chocolates or desserts either. "There is sugar even in the rice we eat," she said. The fridge was stripped of all the good stuff.

But Ms Thomas, my English teacher, did not know that. She had asked us to bring to class a packet of juice or any sweetened drink. We had just read "Making Popsicles" in class and we were going to make popsicles that day.

My fear of getting laughed at for bringing bitter gourd and ginger juice was unfounded. No one did. Ms Thomas remarked that my fresh green apple juice looked a little more green than usual. I didn't see the need to correct her.

We laid out newspapers over the long tables in the canteen for the activity. We poured the juices into moulds carefully. There were six moulds for six popsicles and we were each assigned to one mould. When it was my turn, I accidently spilled a little bit of my juice into Ah Seng's "coconut with pulp" juice. Ah Seng was very proud of the fact that his popsicle would be the only one with juicy bits in it. He didn't notice what I had done then. I thought it was best not to tell him that he now had a coconut with pulp plus bitter gourd and ginger popsicle. Thankfully, when the popsicles were ready four hours later, Ah Seng's popsicle looked rather pretty. He even proudly showed it off to the rest of us. His was the only multicoloured popsicle in the class.

I didn't wait to find out what happened when he ate it. I ran home as fast as I could with my popsicle in hand for my mother. I think she loved it as she stocked up the refrigerator with fruit juices the next day for me. She said it was a reward for making such a lovely popsicle for her and now I could make more. She added that fruit juices made better popsicles than vegetable juices.

The next day, it was time to write about our experience of making popsicles. Ah Seng, Janani, Fatema and I worked together to describe our little activity. Ah Seng thought the popsicles tasted horrible. Janani and Fatema disagreed. They quarrelled for a bit. I did not say anything. I focused on the task at hand. Ms Thomas told us to write about our experience on a large sheet of mahjong paper that was handed to us. I always volunteered to do the writing. I had the best handwriting and was best at spelling in the group. As the group's resident note-taker and writer, I had the responsibility to tidy up their contributions and shape it into something interesting. I liked my role.

We read our stories to the class and Ah Seng was a little sad when everyone vehemently disagreed with him about how the popsicles tasted.

"Maybe your coconut juice with pulp was spoilt. Did you check the expiry date?" asked Ms Thomas, puzzled by the turn of events. Again, I thought it best not to say anything.

The final stage of the writing activity was for us to write individual compositions of 150 words. Ms Thomas had taught us the three stages of narrative structure a few weeks ago: the beginning, the conflict and the resolution. She went through the structure once again.

It was time to write my composition. I wrote about reading "Making Popsicles" in class and being asked to bring in the juice. The conflicts were clear. I had three. The first conflict was that my mother was on yet another diet plan and there was no sweet juice for my activity. The second conflict was that she was always busy grading papers and I could not trouble her to buy me a packet of juice. The third conflict was that I had poured part of the bitter gourd and ginger juice into my classmate's popsicle mould. The resolution was the plan that I had devised to resolve the matter. I had poured my mother's morning breakfast juice into my water bottle and brought it to class, and I had helped my classmate to make a good-looking popsicle by sharing some of my juice rather selflessly. Matter resolved. I also explained how much my mother enjoyed the popsicle that I had made for her as she had eaten it up rather quickly and how I was my classmate, Ah Seng's, "Secret Santa" – you know, the one who "helped" him with his popsicle project.

Having read my work once over carefully, I submitted it to Ms Thomas. But first, I waited until everyone had handed in their papers before I did. It was a little trick I had learned from observing my mother grade papers. When your paper sat on top of a pile of scripts, teachers marked them first. My mother only got tired halfway through the marking. She was always happy when she marked the first script.

As luck would have it, Ms Thomas started marking the compositions in class that day. I watched as she picked mine up first. When she came to the last part of the paper, Ms Thomas started chuckling so loudly that she nearly slipped off her chair.

"Sudiksha, girl ... you can sell ice to an Eskimo with your writing!"

St Xavier's Girls School English Teacher, Ms Seah Chai Suang

I loved teaching at the elite all-girls school. It fulfilled my childhood fantasy of being in Enid Blyton's "The Naughtiest Girl" and "Malory Towers" series that I had read faithfully. St Xavier's Girls School was British – as British as it could be in sweltering Asia. I often remarked with great pride to random strangers whom I spoke to on the train rides home that "St Xavier's Girls is all things British."

I bought all of the school's memorabilia as well and proudly displayed them in my home and on my work desk. It made me feel like I was a St Xavier's alumna myself and not from Angsana Secondary School. I was the only one in my family who had not done well enough in the highly competitive national examinations that all of us took at primary six. The examination determined the type of secondary school we were posted to. Unlike my older sisters, I did not make the cut to attend any elite school because of my poor Mathematics results. I scored a distinction only in English Language. I spent most of my teenage years in my sisters' shadows. But now I was one of them. I, too, had stories to share about my adventures at St Xavier's Girls.

I ensured that the newbies in secondary one were aware of the honour bestowed on them at having been accepted into an upper-crust school that made ladies out of young girls. I paid close attention to their diction, attire and penmanship. The girls in my class had to dot their i's and cross their t's at all times.

"Remember girls, always put your best foot forward! How you carry yourself is a reflection of St Xavier's Girls School. Even if some members of the public say anything derogatory about you, remember to hold your head up and walk away with a smile. They are just envious and know that you come from privileged homes."

It was a school with very few middle-class families. The bulk of the families were from the business community and high-ranking officials who donated generously to all fund-raising events, resulting in much better facilities such as our own swimming pool, auditorium and a first-class gymnasium. Despite all of that, it was gratifying to see that the girls were oblivious to social class differences. Their friendships were not bound by where their peers lived or the type of cars their parents drove. Instead, it was based on whom they sat next to in class and their extra-curricular activities. Most of them also knew one another as they had gone to St Xavier's Primary School or were from the same church.

As the English teacher of the secondary one class, I also had the responsibility of preparing them for the academic rigour expected of a St Xavier's girl. Many girls found the leap from primary to secondary school a rather steep learning curve. This was rather evident in the English language classroom. For instance, many of the girls would have primarily written narratives in their primary schools. But at the secondary school level, they were required to write different types of texts. A letter was a nice way of easing them out of their comfort zone. It had some elements of storytelling and yet a far more rigid structure than a narrative. So out of the three prompts given in the school curriculum, I chose the one that required them to write a letter to someone inviting them over to a surprise party.

I dug up the two letters from my best friend, Angel Sim. Angel and I had promised to write to one another when we were posted to different secondary schools. We didn't have telephones in our homes then. I continued to write for months even after her letters had stopped. Years later, when I ran into her at the university, she had shrugged the whole thing off as being too tiresome.

"It's important to write to people you care about," I stressed to the class. The girls looked puzzled.

"But, Ms Seah, no one writes letters anymore. We just WhatsApp each other. What does a letter look like?" asked the girl seated at the far end of the second row.

"Well, *ladies* do! They put on their best penmanship and use beautiful writing pads for special letters." The girls didn't protest any further.

For the next hour and a half, I taught them the conventions of a good letter, emphasising the need to be persuasive, warm and sincere in the letter. I showed them samples such as my old letters. The girls were intrigued by the pretty paper and the old Singapore stamps that I had brought to class.

"Remember to add details about where the party is, who else is invited and why it is a surprise. Do not write more than 350 words or fewer than 250 words. You have one week for this. Now, don't forget to make the letter interesting. No one is going to come to a boring party."

A week later, the girls dutifully placed their compositions on my table. I did not even have to prompt them. They were a diligent lot. I noticed the Indian girl with long pigtails and broad black-rimmed Harry Potter-like spectacles still clinging on to a clear folder with foolscap paper in it. She kept looking around the room and back at the paper in her hands.

"Ah, this one must not have done her work," I muttered to myself. She was the only Indian girl in the class so it was easy to locate her name on the class register. But I could not get my tongue around it. It was an unusual name with many initials: KVP Sudiksha Menon. Gosh, how does one pronounce a name like that! Maybe the girl had an English name like everyone else in the class. If not, I could give her one like Suzy or Sylvia. A name that starts with the same alphabet as hers would be nice. Teenage girls tend to be attached to the first letter of their name for some reason. They have it monogrammed on their schoolbags, pencil cases and even on their stationery. I will be doing the girl a favour. She will find it easy to fit in with her anglophile classmates.

After all, my own English teacher, Mrs Rahman, had also given me an English name, Christine, when she could not pronounce Chai Suang.

Sudiksha Menon's Mother, Sushila Nair

My little one was little no more. She was all of 13 this year. She had grown taller over the December holidays but, thankfully, she had not filled out in all the right places or the wrong places yet. But there was time for that.

I spent my evenings listening to her tell me "grown up" stories about Geography and History classes. These were a novelty to her as they are only introduced at the secondary school level. For Sudiksha, the classes provided research material for the stories she scribbled away furiously in her writing journal.

"I am going to be a historical fiction writer," she declared one day.

"What's a historical fiction writer? You mean a writer who writes about Mahathir and Lee Kuan Yew?" quipped my father.

"Huh, nooooooo, *Appuppa*.[1] It will be like stories where my characters live in a different time period or location. I will describe their lives and the things they do and use historical events in the background."

"Oh, like those historical love stories with that fellow Fabio Lanzoni with very little clothes on the book cover? Sometimes there is a woman with him on the cover. She, too, would have long hair and very little clothes on her. Your mother loved those stories."

---

1 Grandfather in Malayalam.

"*Accha*!"[2] I could not believe my ears. What was he telling the little one!

"Ewww ... *Amma*,[3] you read those sexy books?" asked Sudiksha, giving me a once-over. I didn't have the heart to tell her that I had read Sidney Sheldon's "If Tomorrow Comes" when I was 11 years old. I had received a thrashing from my late mother for having ventured into her secret stash of books. Sigh! Sudiksha must think of me as a straight-laced mother. Well, I was once a teenager, too. But that was a lifetime ago.

"It's true. Your mother ... my daughter ..." he added, emphasising "my daughter", "... spent a lot of money – my money – buying those books from Sunny Bookstore at Far East Plaza in those days."

I covered my face with my hands. It didn't look like my father was going to stop any time soon.

"Now she hides them in the old suitcase under her bed. Yes, ... yes, *Mole*,[4] you write those. You can make lots of money from that. We can make back what your mother spent on those books."

My father chuckled heartily, oblivious to the discomfort he had caused. By now, Sudiksha and I had turned beetroot-red.

Sudiksha took out the dinner plates on her own accord and laid the table. I hurried into the kitchen to see to dinner.

The silence in the room must have put my father in a pensive mood.

"You know, Sudiksha *Kutti*,[5] you are very lucky. Your primary school English teacher was always encouraging you to write. She came up with so many creative things for you guys. Didn't you want to be a National Geographic writer last year? You wrote that piece about bugs, or was it elephants, for your class? What was it? *Appuppa* forgot."

---

2   Dad in Malayalam.
3   Mother in Malayalam.
4   Daughter in Malayalam.
5   Baby in Malayalam.

The silence in the room prevailed.

"I wasn't so lucky," continued my father. "One of my teachers called me a liar. She even wrote that on my compo. I was only nine years old!"

"But why, *Appuppa*?" whispered Sudiksha, unable to fathom such cruelty from an adult.

"Well, we were asked to describe our neighbourhood. I wrote about my *kampong*[6] in Sembawang. I described the Naval Base shipyard, the shops in Chong Pang and the Sembawang Hot Springs. I had written, "Many people from all over the world visit the Sembawang Hot Springs.""

"What's wrong with that?" I asked. I had heard that it was a tourist spot in the 1960s and 1970s.

"Yes. I always saw a lot of white people there. Families from the Naval Base and their friends. I was only nine years old. I thought that meant that people from all over the world visited the Hot Springs. But the teacher …"

He paused. He was visibly upset.

"The teacher wrote 'Liar! Why are you lying like this?' on my compo in red pen. Never mind that – when she was giving out the compos to the class, she yelled out, 'BV Krishna Nair, don't write lies in your compo!' I thought I was going to die of shame that day."

Sudiksha moved closer to him and rested her hand on his. He held her hand and gazed at it for a moment before continuing.

"Not the only time, you know. When *Appuppa* was 12 years old – that's just one year younger than you are now – my English teacher asked me to write a story about the ideal house that I would like to live in. I lived at 13th Mile Sembawang, where there was no electricity or running water. We studied under the light from kerosene lamps in those days. So I wrote that my ideal home was a beautiful semi-detached terrace house surrounded by

---

6   Village in Malay.

fruit trees in a nice part of town. I also said that the neighbours there would be well-educated and well-heeled, and they would hold high-ranking positions in the civil service."

I could not see where this was going. It sounded like a typical composition that a child would have written.

"I had even looked up the spelling of 'well-educated' and 'well-heeled' in a dictionary, to see if there was a hyphen in each word. You know what the teacher wrote? In capital letters, she wrote, 'ARE YOU WELL-EDUCATED AND WELL-HEELED YOURSELF?'"

His voice broke. The impact of the teacher's words still had this man tearing 60 years later.

13-year-old Sudiksha Menon

I skipped back to my table with a broad smile plastered on my face.

Ms Seah stared at me for a few moments with a quizzical look before turning her attention to the pile of compositions on her table. She started counting the papers. I knew that she was keeping track of the submissions. It was a commonly known fact that students who forgot to turn in their homework would wait to be discovered.

As luck would have it, my composition did catch her attention. She picked it up and flipped through it. I could see that my script was bulkier than the rest in the pile. She quickly turned it back to check the name on the first page.

I waited for her to smile with satisfaction as Ms Thomas always did when she read my composition. I was bursting to tell her that I wanted to be a writer when I grew up – a writer who won many awards and was featured in the press.

"Su-it-cha, come here! Why did you paste a family photo in your letter? For heaven's sake, will you be able to stick a photo in your compo during the exams?"

With that, Ms Seah yanked off the photograph from the foolscap paper and handed the offending piece of paper to me. The force with which she had attacked it tore the photograph, leaving only a small part of it still on the foolscap paper. It was a stubborn piece indeed. Ms Seah could not pull it out.

I noticed that my grandfather's face was torn in half. My grandaunt's face was still stuck to the foolscap paper. Fighting back the tears in my eyes, I quickly stuffed the offending piece of paper into the bottom of my schoolbag and stared at the whiteboard.

The teacher continued the lesson on letter writing and how to communicate effectively.

Author's Note

"Voices" is dedicated to all the writing teachers whom I have taught over the years. We have debated over what a writing teacher should value most, the writer or the text, and the implications of giving emphasis to only one element in the classroom, *ad nauseum*. Both are important elements, of course. I wrote this story as a cautionary tale for my fellow writing teachers to examine the subtle things that we say and do in the classroom that can empower and create the next Ernest Hemingway or nip the spirit of a potential young writer in its bud.

I chose a non-linear narrative structure for the story to show a contrast across different writing classrooms and teachers that Sudhiksha Menon encountered in her life. Often when we say or do things, we are not privy to the recipient's life nor do we know the impact of the words on the recipient. This structure also provided me with a means to provide a backstory to Ms Seah. I often write backstories for the characters that I create but rarely include them into the narratives. However, I felt compelled to reveal Ms

Seah's life. We are, after all, made up of our dreams and experiences, and Ms Seah deserved to have her story told. The non-linear narrative structure helped me to achieve this, and I have added headings to avoid confusing the reader.

The title "Voices" was a natural fit for what I wanted to achieve. There are three main protagonists in this story and the three stories are told from their perspectives. It's their voices that you hear as they narrate their memories and their stories. I envisioned this text being read by actors in these four roles: 9-year-old Sudhiksha, 13-year-old Sudhiksha, Mrs Seah and Sushila.

To further achieve the purpose of each distinctive voice in the story, I wrote each segment to stand alone as an independent narrative that can be read without reference to the other segments. Each segment tells a little story on its own. When the segments are put together, the larger picture emerges, enabling the reader to fully realise the impact of the story.

The Young Fan

Raymund P Reyes

Every generation of teenagers idolises pop music boy bands that define not only the youngsters' taste in music but also their choices in areas such as fashion, attitudes, outlook, even food. From the Beatles in the 1960s to New Kids on the Block in the 1980s and One Direction in the 2000s, their millions of fans have invested time and money to ensure that their celebrity idols remain in the limelight and increase their album sales. To the fans, the longevity of their favourite band's celebrity status justifies their fandom.

BTS is the boy band of the moment. Thanks to the millions of young fans in the Asian diaspora who are largely responsible for the band's rise to prominence, the rest of the world has not been able to ignore this septet of singing and dancing boys from South Korea. Their fans saturate social media with their expressions of adulation for the band, buying records and merchandise to ensure that their latest releases shoot to the top of music charts not only in Asia but also in Europe and America. BTS has made teenagers in the West listen to (and love) music that they can barely understand, and in the process getting them curious about K-pop, Korean drama, *Hangul*,[1] *hallyu*[2] and *bibimbap*.[3] The Philippines have not been spared from the BTS craze. Filipino teenage girls, in particular, have always been big fans of boy bands, and while they may have preferred American and British acts not too long ago, they are now screaming and swooning over a proudly Asian group.

"Where can I find the magazines?" Eleven-year-old Ginny asked the sales clerk who was bent over by the bottom shelf of the aisle

---

1 The alphabet or writing system of the Korean language.

2 Also known as the "Korean wave", it refers to the global rise in popularity of South Korean culture.

3 A Korean rice dish topped with a variety of vegetables, chilli paste, meat and often a raw or fried egg.

nearest the drugstore entrance, straightening boxes of cleaners, toners and moisturisers. Ginny knew she could find the magazine aisle herself but she had no time to browse. Her mother was waiting for her in the car outside as she had promised to just grab the magazine she wanted and be done as fast as she could.

"Right there," the sales clerk said as she stood up and pointed to a rack of books and magazines beside the front cash counters a few aisles away. "Are you looking for a particular magazine?"

"Do you have the BTS magazine?" Ginny asked.

"Is BTS the name of the magazine?" The clerk had a quizzical look on her face as she accompanied Ginny toward the display of books and magazines. "I don't think I've heard of it before."

"No, it's not the magazine's name. BTS is like the best and greatest K-pop boy band ever," the girl giggled and blushed. "It's a special issue."

"I think I know which one you're looking for. The one with the weird-looking boys on the cover. Oh, I'm sorry," the sales clerk slapped her forehead gently and looked at the young girl apologetically when she realised the customer was serious about her expression of admiration. "Me and my big mouth."

"Oh, that's all right, Miss," Ginny said. "I know what you mean. Many people say the same thing about the group. But they are famous all over the world and everyone who loves K-pop knows their songs by heart. If you get to know them, you might love them, too. They are so unique and so good-looking and … I'm just such a fan!"

"Oh, I understand, honey," the sales clerk said as she started scanning the rows of magazine titles that lined an entire wall of the drugstore. "I think I dig your enthusiasm. During my time, when I was your age, it was NSYNC and the Backstreet Boys. I would also buy magazines with them on the cover. My mom thought I was crazy."

"There it is! There it is!" The girl squealed in delight as she pointed to a magazine on the bottom rack.

The cover screamed *BTS* in all caps, the yellow letters set against a bubblegum pink background; and below in smaller type, *2020 Special Collector's Edition*. Splashed dead-centre on the cover were seven young Asian boys, comprising the boy band which the young girl idolised. They looked like ordinary well-dressed teenagers going to a prom in black suits and bow ties, except for the unusual colouring of their hair – obviously dyed – which clashed with their pale skin. Two band members had different shades of brown with highlights, one boy sported grey hair, another was blonde, while yet another was a brunette. The sixth member had dyed his hair green, while the last one sported a purple mop. And all of them were obviously wearing bright pink lipstick. The magazine cover promised two fold-out posters inside, fun trivia about the group, an article about the band members' biggest dreams, upcoming collaborations with other artistes, and even psychic predictions for the New Year.

"There you go! I'm glad we have copies. Enjoy!" The clerk smiled at the young customer before turning to walk away.

"Thank you so much," the girl replied, but her eyes were transfixed on the magazine she was holding like a sacred relic in her two hands, which were shaking from pure excitement and the realisation that she was actually about to own a copy of the coveted magazine. Ginny knew it was coming out that day. She and a few classmates, all avid fans of the same boy band, had been talking about this special issue. Online fan groups had been promoting it on Facebook, Instagram and fan sites, making sure that every member of the BTS Army, as the fans called themselves, would know about the newest publication dedicated to their K-pop idols to be exclusively released in Southeast Asia. The classmates had promised to buy and read the magazine over the weekend as it was going to be on their agenda for discussion over lunch on Monday (and perhaps the entire week at school). Ginny was glad she and her mother went out to buy their groceries that Saturday. If she had waited until the next day, no more copies would have been left on the shelf of any bookstore or drugstore in Metro Manila because any merchandise that featured the boy band was bound to sell like hotcakes.

When Ginny reached the front cash counter, there were two customers ahead of her. An old lady who was currently paying for her purchases had a full cart to unload. As she waited for her turn in the queue, Ginny fought the urge to flip through the pages and have a peek inside. There was no way she was going to rush the reading of this magazine. She would take her time going through every photograph and article, making sure she did not miss an inch of every picture, every juicy detail about her favourite boy band revealed in every sentence and paragraph. She had probably watched all videos featuring BTS on YouTube, Instagram and other social media sites and links that she and her classmates exchanged during lunch and after school. She would Google for articles and updates about the K-pop group every day. She was even learning the Korean language on the sly because she hoped one day to be able to stop relying on the subtitles in those videos. She believed the translations did not fully capture the meaning of whatever was being said in Korean.

Ginny was careful, however, to keep her mother clueless about her addiction to BTS. If her mother knew that each time she was logged into the Internet at home she was doing more research on BTS than studying, she would be in trouble. All her mother knew was that she was a fan of the boy band. Songs in a language which nobody in the family could understand blared constantly from her room. Her mother didn't know that Ginny did not only love to listen to BTS music, she also wanted to learn about the most trivial things she could about the boys, such as Jungkook's favourite colour, what Jimin would love to eat for breakfast, and what Jin, her secret crush among them, would be looking for in a girlfriend.

"I just need to scan that ... Miss?" The cashier asked Ginny when he noticed that the girl could not tear her eyes off the magazine she was holding.

"I'm a fan!" Ginny exclaimed, as she handed over the magazine and a 200-peso bill to the cashier.

"I understand," the cashier smiled. "We have someone who works at the store who's also a big fan. She just spent 10,000 pesos for a concert ticket and maxed out her credit card. We all think she's crazy, but I guess we are all crazy about something so I don't want to judge her for what she did. Do you know that they're coming to Manila next year?"

"Yes, of course," Ginny answered. "The fan sites are all talking about it. Unfortunately, I'm too young to go. And even if I could, I don't think I'd be able to afford it. When I'm older, I'm going to get a job and the first thing I'd be saving for is a ticket to watch BTS in concert."

"How old are you?" the cashier asked.

"Eleven."

"Do you think they'd still be popular ten years from now?"

"They'll be famous forever!" Ginny answered confidently.

The cashier laughed at the young girl. "Well, enjoy," he said, as he handed the magazine back to Ginny along with a receipt.

"Oh, thank you. I will," Ginny replied, her voice almost breaking. She looked down self-consciously as she tried to fight the tears that were then threatening to embarrass her in front of the cashier.

* * *

A heavyset woman in her late 30s, her hair dyed flaming red, rushed into the drugstore and proceeded to the front cash counter, carrying in her hand the same BTS magazine that Ginny had purchased earlier.

"Excuse me, Sir. My daughter was here a few minutes ago. She bought this." She put the magazine on top of the glass-topped counter along with the receipt. "I would like to return it and get a refund, please."

"Of course, Ma'am. Is there a problem with it? Missing or torn pages?" the cashier asked the woman.

"No, it's not the pages," she answered. "It's the magazine itself. I think it's ridiculous! That kid! I thought when she said she wanted to rush inside to buy some magazine, she was referring to something school-related, something educational like *Time*, *National Geographic* or something. But look at these pale-faced Asian men wearing makeup and colourful hair! She tried to hide it when she got in the car but I insisted on having a look and I'm glad I did. I don't get what she likes about this BTS band. You can't even understand half of what they're saying."

"I don't get them either, Ma'am," the cashier replied. "But they must be the most popular boy band in the world right now. Even the girls in my class – and these are college students, mind you – are mad about them."

"I must have tolerated her craziness for this K-pop thing for far too long. I mean, every generation has its own taste and understandably, since I come from another generation, I would not get the appeal of these strange-looking young men. I know it's just like how my parents could not get why I loved the Backstreet Boys in my youth. I believe as long as it's reasonable and being a fan doesn't make you do crazy things, then why not indulge? But this time, I told my kid she's gone beyond sanity for spending 200 pesos for this darn magazine right here! I could buy lunch in McDonald's for both of us with that same amount of money and get some change left over."

The cashier grinned at the indignant mother before him, but when he looked out of the store, he caught a glance of the daughter, looking back at them from the window of the car parked by the sidewalk. Tears glistened in her eyes, but unlike earlier, this time they were not tears of joy.

Author's Note

I went over to the books and magazines section of a drugstore and saw a young girl seated cross-legged on the floor, poring over a magazine devoted entirely to the K-pop boy band, BTS. She was so absorbed in her reading, she *ooh-ed* and *aah-ed* at intervals, as if she had retreated into her own world right there in the corner of the store. I scooted nearer, my curiosity piqued as to what was consuming this youngster's interest. She was reading an article about one of the boy band members' comfort food. The spread featured colourful graphics, a collage of photos and a recipe. A wicked thought occurred to me just then: What if I suddenly snatched that magazine out of her hands? Her reaction would be a story, I thought. I imagined describing her face like a final close-up shot in a movie before it blacks out.

With already a germ of a plot and an ending, I spent most of the pre-writing stage fleshing out a story about a young protagonist who thought she had already gotten what she wanted, only for the prize to be taken away. There are various ways to advance such a plot. The writer may prepare the reader by placing clues at various points of the story so that when the rug is finally pulled out from under the character's feet, the ending would be expected and inevitable. Or everything could seem to go fine for the main character until a surprise twist occurs in just one sentence or paragraph, where he or she is denied a happy ending.

I divided my story into two parts. The first part focuses on the protagonist's triumph. After going through the agony that goes with expecting something good to happen, Ginny finally lays her hands on the BTS magazine. The second part negates the joy of the first half. Ginny's mother returns the magazine to the store, thereby making the young girl sad and disappointed.

The girl does not appear in the second section except at the very end, where I place the close-up shot that I had envisioned prior to actually writing the story. The image is identical to the section that ends the first part where the girl is also on the verge of tears. However, the emotions of the character in the two instances are opposites.

The Last Bullock Cart in Town

Babitha Marina Justin

About 30 years ago, Thiruvananthapuram, the capital of Kerala, was endowed with the beauty and naiveté of a small town. Caste was a major factor which divided the society. Though people did not speak about it, they had it in their minds. Very few people were insulated from it, and the ones who were insulated were society's privileged. It infiltrated everywhere. Schools nurtured hierarchy and never questioned it. Many children from the non-privileged castes suffered in this system as it hampered their progress.

As the town embraced modernity, many symbols of tradition and old ways of living harmoniously with nature disappeared or were erased altogether. Modernity swept over farmlands and swamps. For instance, bullock carts and traditional ways of farming became a memory. By 1990, due to globalisation and opening up of markets, the small town rapidly turned into a satellite town. Today, interestingly, the individual parts of a bullock cart can be seen as museum installations in art galleries. Along with it, caste discrimination, too, seems to have taken a backseat.

Kerala, 1985

As the Ambassador car honked impatiently at her gate, Rati wolfed down her *dosa*[1] rolled up with peanut chutney. A piece of *dosa* got stuck, and she almost choked on it. Her mother hit the crown of her head a couple of times and thrust a glass of water at her. She took a gulp, swallowed the chunk in her throat while her eyes swept over the sofa, cabinets and tables on the veranda.

"Where is my school tie?" She mumbled with her mouth still full of *dosa*.

---

1 A thin, savoury pancake made from a fermented batter of ground rice and black gram flour.

The driver honked again, this time angrily. A car full of faces, polished, powdered and shocked out of their dreams, were being carted to school.

"He will start shouting now," Rati murmured to herself as she rummaged through her books and emptied the laundry basket to look for the tie.

"Hey, you idiot child, we are going to be late again! If you don't come out in a second, we will leave without you!"

The whirlwind search for the tie, upsetting the books and pulling out her clothes from her trunk and laundry basket stopped. Rati saw her dirty school tie peeping out of her bag.

She sighed, it was smelly and creased, but the tie would have to do. She picked up her school bag and ran to the car. By the time she came panting and huffing to the gate, the driver had revved up the car and sped off. She saw the Ambassador turn the corner of her road in a cloud of dust and vanish like a white elephant. She ran behind it, staggering under the weight of her Duckback.[2]

"Driver uncle, stop! Please stop!" She cried out.

The car gathered speed. She knew that the driver wanted to teach her a lesson. She was late almost every day. There was not a single day she had not struggled with time, studies, her teachers and friends. Rati sank down to her knees on the road and wept. This was the only vehicle which went to the school, which was a few miles away. There was not another single moving thing in sight that she could hitch-hike to school in her little town. If she went back home, she would get a nice spanking from her mother. Every day, her mother tried to wake her up early, but she loved to cuddle for a little while longer under her blanket until the sun crept up on her face. And by then, it was already time for school.

Each morning, her mother picked her up from the bed, took her to the bathroom and downed a copper pot full of water on

2 A popular brand of schoolbags in India.

her head. A cold waterfall shook her body, her teeth chattered, and she shut her eyes tight while the empty pot clanged on the granite floor. She stood there, shivering and shifting her feet on the floor. Her mother held her down, and she smelled the gentle scent of Rexona as she was soaped all over her goose-pimpled skin. Whenever she soaped Rati's face, Rati crinkled her eyes to catch a glimpse of sunlight sifting through the bubbly suds. Her eyes smarted, and she splashed water on her face.

"Stand still, Rati!" Another pot of water was poured over her. Her mother wrapped her up in a towel, carried her to the veranda and dried her. Rati's bones rattled after the cold shower. She did a little dance to warm her bones, hopping and wobbling on the wet floor, punching her arms and legs sideways.

Rati could not go back home. She wiped her eyes and nose with her tie, and thought of walking to school. If she took a short cut through the swamp, that would be easier, she thought. She walked through the mud path, jumping over puddles and picking thorny thistles off her pinafore. From behind, she heard gentle bells and wheels rolling over gutters. She turned back to see the silhouette of a bullock cart trundling its way across the purple mist that blanketed the swamp. To Rati, it looked like a picture-perfect paradise for a moment. Two proud and majestic bulls pulled the cart, and their horns arched over the horizon.

The cart rolled on as she moved towards the edge of the path, balancing on her feet so that she did not fall into the slush.

"Missed your car, child?" The bullock cart driver hollered at her.

Rati nodded, scrunching her face.

"Hop in! I am going that way, it will take a while, but you won't be late." Rati hesitated for a moment. Her parents would scold her if they knew about this, but who would ever tell them? She was both thrilled and wary at the prospect of a bullock cart ride. She always loved the lazy, trundling pace in which it clattered on broken tarmac.

"Thank you, *Maama*."[3] She threw her Duckback and water bottle into the cart, and clambered in. There were sacks full of freshly harvested vegetables, and she inhaled the aroma of home-grown ridge gourd. She loved the way her mother shallow fried it with ginger, bird's eye chillies and mashed shallots. The sky shone a golden ring of sunbeam on her. She noticed a sliver of a stork standing single-legged in the marsh, watching out for fish.

"Are these vegetables from your garden?" She asked the bullock cart driver, poking at a swollen pumpkin.

"Not mine, my neighbours sell them to me, and I take them to the market," he replied, cracking the whip in the air.

"What is your name, *Maama*? I am Rati." She asked him as the cart rolled on. She counted four storks and spotted a cormorant in the distance. It was a rickety, bone-shattering ride, but Rati began to enjoy every moment.

"I know you. You are Meena *Chechi's*[4] daughter, aren't you? My name is Kesavan, and these boys are Raman and Laxman." He said without turning back and pointing his whip at the two handsome bulls.

"Are they twins?" she asked, looking at their shimmering backs, their limbs moving rhythmically with their backs. Their tails hung down and bunched into fistfuls of hair.

"They are brothers. Raman, the one on the right, with a black mole on his haunch, is the elder one." He tapped the bullocks gently with his whip. Their tails twitched and rippled at his touch.

"Do they attack strangers?" Rati felt a strong urge to touch them.

"They are friendly when I am around. You can touch them if you want, when you get down." Rati flashed a smile at Kesavan when he looked back at her fondly.

---

3 Uncle in Malayalam, a term used by children to address older gentlemen.
4 Elder or older sister in Malayalam.

"What made you wake up so late and miss the car?" Kesavan tucked his whip under his arm and removed the *thorthu*[5] he had tied as his headgear. He uncoiled the *thorthu* and shook it out. His sweat beads sprayed around like droplets of pearls in the mild sunlight.

"I woke up late." Rati watched Kesavan re-tie his *thorthu* on his head with his whip still tucked under his arm.

"Why, *Mole*?"[6] Kesavan's voice was tender and caring. Somehow, she didn't want to disappoint him by saying that she was too lazy to wake up early. Not batting an eyelid, she said: "No one loves me at home, so I wake up late."

To her surprise, Kesavan laughed, throwing his head back.

"Ha ha, what strange reason is that?" he asked, still laughing. His brown muscles gleamed and rippled with laughter.

"What is strange?" Rati pouted, gazing at the parrot green paddy stalks nodding their mocking heads from the marsh. She understood that this sentiment would not curry favour with him.

A moment later, she confessed in a whisper: "I am not good at studies. I hate going to school."

"Is that so?" Kesavan turned back again, his forehead creased.

"Not only that …" Rati's voice trailed and she focused her gaze on the cormorant. Its blackness stood out amidst the blanket petals of white storks. It sat still for a long while and then sprang up in a swift movement and dove down into the green thistles bordering the swamp. It emerged from the green, propelling itself, rocketing up and perching on a black stump with a struggling fish in its beak.

"I have no friends at school." Rati managed to blurt out despite her voice thickening with grief.

"Why, child?"

---

5   A thin, white cotton towel in Malayalam.

6   Daughter in Malayalam, also an affectionate term used to address young girls.

"My classmates don't let me play with them." With a few jerking moves, the cormorant swallowed the fish and sat sagacious after the hearty meal. Two big teardrops itched to squeeze out of Rati's eyes.

To her disbelief, Kesavan coughed at first and then peals of laughter rang out in the air.

Her eyes widened, watching him convulsed with laughter.

"You find it funny?" she pushed her lower lip forward.

"No, no. I laughed because nowadays kids have such strange excuses to stay away from school," he said, still laughing. "You think it's an excuse?" Rati's face reddened.

Kesavan was silent for some time, then cleared his throat.

"Child, let me tell you the story of a bullock cart. My father told me this story when I refused to go back to school after fifth grade." The older bull cocked his ears and shook his harness bells.

"Raman wants to listen, too." Kesavan laughed, showing a set of betel leaf stained teeth.

"A long time ago, there was a bullock cart like mine, and one day, all parts of the cart started quarrelling. The wheels creaked, 'We are big and round, and we pull things along, so we are the most important.' The sledge pole squeaked, 'I am strong, and I tie you to the bulls, so I am more important.' At last, the little lynchpin spoke up: 'Without me, both of you would fall apart. Without me, you cannot run the cart.'"

Kesavan stopped for a while and sighed, looking mistily at the nodding paddy fields, and then whistled to the bulls. They started climbing a hillock from where they could see a winding road. Rati's school was at the end of the winding road. She felt a strange sadness grip her heart as the cart approached the school.

"I didn't realise the importance of this story until my parents passed on, and when they were gone, I realised my wheels and pole bars were gone, too. My world fell apart."

Kesavan mopped his sweaty face with his *thorthu* when he reached the end of the road. When they stopped at the school, Kesavan ferreted out a shiny guava fruit and handed it over to Rati.

"Take this, child, this is the first fruit from the youngest guava tree in the yard. The smallest and youngest tree never understands it, but it is as worthy as the tallest and oldest tree in the world."

The bullock cart rolled away, rattling noisily on the road. Though she was late for school, a strange wave of happiness swept over her.

The next day, Rati prised open her eyes before the sun showed up, and bathed and dressed on her own. Her mother was wide-eyed with surprise. She waited for her school car near her gate. When the car came to a wobbly halt near her, she saw the distant glimpse of a bullock cart rolling towards her and shouted to the driver over the drone of the engine.

"I will come back with you only in the evening; my uncle is dropping me off to school."

The other children in the car looked at her with large, apprehensive eyes, wondering where this new uncle had dropped from the sky. She pulled her collar up and gave them a smart nod and a wink as the driver muttered something under his breath and stepped on the accelerator.

Rati could see the bullock cart trundling by with its clatter and bells. Without even asking Kesavan for permission, Rati threw her bag in and hopped into the cart. She pulled out a carrot fragrant with the smell of the earth from a sack.

"Do rabbits eat fresh carrots like these?" Rati wanted to know, as she bit into its crisp freshness.

"Yes, they do. Have you missed your car again?" Kesavan raised his eyebrows in mock surprise.

"No. I like this bumpy ride, and I want you to tell me your stories. It's so boring in the jam-packed car. Our driver is surly, and he scolds us when we talk."

Kesavan threw his head back and laughed. He turned around and asked her, half in jest, "You aren't going to make this a habit, are you?"

"Ummm, no. Not really, Kesavan *Maama*. But, maybe, I can keep you company once in a while," she said, twisting the jute threads that hemmed the vegetable sack.

Kesavan guffawed. A few storks took offence and looked at him sharply.

"Why did you stop going to school, *Maama*?" asked Rati, pulling out another carrot.

"It is a long story, a rather unpleasant one." Kesavan shook his head.

"Tell me, please, *Maama*." Rati bit off the head of the carrot and spat it out.

"I was born in a colony of potters called Velakkudi. My father had a small farm and he moved away from pottery. He tilled the land, planted a variety of crops and built a small house away from the colony. He worked hard and we lived a comfortable life." Holding the reins loosely, Kesavan touched his eyes with his left hand. He hurried Raman and Laxman by swishing the whip and swirling it in the air.

Hearing the whip, the crows resting on the fringes of the farm started, took flight and scattered their downy feathers on the ground.

"I was admitted to a government school. There were all kinds of children there. I was the only *Velan*[7] and I was very dark and poor."

Kesavan stretched out an arm. She saw the different shades of blue, purple, magenta and deep brown glimmer on his dark skin.

---

7   A person belonging to the potter caste in Kerala.

"They threw me out of the class!" Kesavan guffawed.

"The boys from better homes and the upper castes did not like me sitting with them in the classroom. So, the teachers asked me to stand at the door and listen. I listened to the classes and when my legs ached, I squatted down and wrote down everything the teachers taught. One day, a teacher took pity on me and gave me a seat in the corner, away from the other boys."

Rati gazed at his firm grasp on the reins and his brown knuckles which gleamed in the sun. Kesavan continued, "The boys also complained that I smelled, I had only one uniform which I washed and used every day, so I was happy to sit in the dark corner." Kesavan's smile had vanished. His eyes held a faraway look.

"Ah, that's why you didn't want to go back to school," Rati said. She caught a whiff of dried cow dung in the air. She didn't turn her face away. It smelled like the swamp; she embraced it by inhaling deeply. Her mother often complained that the servants at home smelled. Rati loved their smell, betel juice mingled with coconut oil and Cuticura talcum powder. They pulled her into their warm fold, saying she looked just like one of them, perhaps a few shades darker. They rested their chins on their palms, clucked sympathetically and wondered, "Where did she get this dark skin from? Meena *Chechi* is so fair and pretty. Poor Rati will not find a suitable boy when she grows up."

They made sure that she was within earshot when they talked about her. They were fond of her, no doubt, but her complexion was one of the secret weapons they used against her fussing, fastidious mother.

"I didn't hate school in the beginning, in fact, I loved going to school and I also started studying well. When I was in fifth grade, I topped the class. My classmates, whose fathers used to hire my father for manual labour occasionally, felt resentful about that.

They complained to the teacher. The teacher supported me.

'Kesavan is a bright boy, I won't entertain any more of your caste tantrums.' She told them firmly. I saw one of them flash a look at me and grind his teeth. He wagged his finger at me in a warning.

One day, when I reached school, some of my classmates were waiting for me. My heart beat fast watching them stand there with folded arms. When I stepped into the school premises, I felt their strong arms grip and drag me to the bathroom. I remember the weight of their punches landing all over my body and I doubled up in pain. Something oozed out of my nose. It tasted of metal and salt on my tongue.

'*Velan's* stinking blood,' I heard them scoff.

'Blood!' I screamed, horrified, as I watched the beetroot patches spread over my uniform like algae in the monsoon.

The next thing I knew was a hand clasping my mouth shut. I struggled as two sweaty arms grappled and pinned me from behind. Something sharp hit me in the eye. I dropped down, pulling down the boy who had grabbed me from behind. The boy on top of me twisted my arms and pinned me down with his knees. Another boy held my neck firmly on the ground, and another started tugging at my uniform."

Kesavan narrated it as if it were a stunt scene in a movie. He scratched his chin and continued.

'Please don't tear my uniform, that's the only one I have,' I cried out, as an arm scraped my face on the ground.

I felt the buttons snap one by one and at last they managed to tear off my uniform and drag it into the mud mixed with urine." Kesavan stared at the rheumy clouds puffing up on a lead sky.

Rati thought of her own ordeals at school. None of those were as bad as Kesavan's.

"I didn't go to school after that. My parents pleaded with me. My teachers tried to coax me back to school, but I was too scared to go. I didn't understand where so much hatred came from," Kesavan sighed. Both the bulls cocked their ears and swished their tails.

"But I survived, I worked hard, bought two bulls, built a house and got married." He craned his neck to look back at her, grinned and winked.

"And I will join you on your rides to the city." Rati beamed back at him.

Kesavan was silent for a while.

"No, dear, this is my last ride to the city," he said, looking at the horizon dreamily. Rati gaped at him with an open mouth. "Why?"

"The corporation won't allow bullock carts on the tarmac roads again. Mine is the last bullock cart in town. I can only drive my cart in the swamp and on mud roads." Kesavan pulled the reins and whistled at Raman and Laxman to hurry up.

He wiggled on his seat and sat upright. With one hand gripping the reins, he scratched his back with the tip of his whip.

"But I will survive. That's what I do when life drags me down." He nodded to no one in particular.

The rest of the journey went by in silence. Rati felt a strange heaviness in her heart. She sulked and looked around at the world accusingly. She had just started enjoying her school ride and her school days. What a killjoy this municipal corporation was.

Kesavan looked at the distant clouds. This smart little bundle of joy called Rati, who had swept over his life for two days, felt unreal. He didn't have children, and he had warmed up to her instantly. That morning, he had even hoped that she would miss her car again. And as if by magic, there she was.

From the next day onwards, Kesavan could only travel by bullock cart within the village limits. He knew with a pang that the end of an era was near. Soon, he would have to sell his handsome bulls, and the last bullock cart in town would become a pretty and useless artefact in a museum. The planks, wheels and the screws would rust in a varnished corner of the world, ruing their bygone bone-rattling days.

Kesavan sighed as he stopped his cart at the school gate. Rati slipped down and walked towards the bulls. This time, Raman and Laxman looked at her with friendly eyes, shaking their bells a little. Rati, by instinct, stroked their muzzles.

"Study well, dear. This is my last drive to the city, and you are my last and best co-passenger," he smiled through a blur of tears, his voice shaking.

"You have the best vehicle in the entire world, and you are the best storyteller. Your stories are just like mine." Her lips trembled, and her eyes filled with large drops of tears.

"Don't cry, dear child. My father used to say that pain is the greatest messenger. Whenever you cry, an angel will bring you a handful of cheer."

Kesavan handed her a bunch of Indian cherries, red and dew fresh.

She walked into the school with leaden steps. She could hear the hooves, the wheels, the sledge bar and the lynchpin creak in unison, crackling on their hinges and getting ready to go. They had to keep moving together until their world fell apart.

Through her tears, she looked at the bunch of cherries in her hand. They reflected a new world and nudged her to move on.

Author's Note

"The Last Bullock Cart" is from a trace of my memory. As a young child growing up in the suburbs, I used to watch the last bullock cart in town trundling by, with its load of vegetables, sacks of rice and, sometimes, heaps of coconut husks. I was enamoured by the clattering, slow-moving cart, and I always fancied a ride on it. But I realised from the rumours around that everyone feared the dark and stern-looking cart driver. Girls scampered away when he looked at us, and boys catcalled and fled. One day, the town planners banned bullock carts on tarred roads and we never saw the cart driver after that. This story is my adult apology to the man who did no harm to us, but was someone whom we dreaded just because he looked different and stern, and was, perhaps, from another caste.

To start writing the story, I had to recreate the suburb where I lived almost 35 years ago. I lived close to a swamp, swathed by small ponds and green fields, and some of the land had coconut groves where we used to hang out and fly kites in the afternoons with our pets. There was a puddle, a narrow *kuccha* (mud) road which ran through the swamp and connected it to the main road which went to the market and school. Remembering these details was an exercise in recalling my memories, as the entire landscape of my neighbourhood had transformed beyond recognition. There is no trace of the swamp now, instead, there is a six-lane bypass with relentless traffic blaring all night and day.

After remembering the childhood landscape, the next process was to get into the skin of the child protagonist, Rati. As I grew up as a dyslexic child who missed classes, taxis and failed in many subjects, it was not very difficult to imagine Rati. I remembered some fine points of my childhood, like losing my tie every day and wiping my nose on it. These elements helped me to add details to the story. The rickety ride I took on bullock carts many years later in northern India also helped to provide details for the bullock cart ride. I outlined the story and finished it in a single sitting, feeling remorseful about the nasty prejudices and colourism with which I grew up. I was writing an apology note for "Kesavan", whom we all dreaded in our childhood. When I wrote this piece, I realised that a younger me, like Rati, would have found great friendship with Kesavan and his two bulls.

Mirror, Mirror

Sachiko Kashiwaba

Translated by Avery Fischer Udagawa

First published in Japanese as "Kagami yo, kagami" in *Mirakuru famirii* (*Miracle Family*, Kodansha Ltd, 2010).

In Japan, gender roles are famously distinct in traditional families. Men often expect to serve as breadwinners, working long hours outside the home, while women frequently shoulder domestic responsibilities. Men and women's comportment, parenting styles, and even speech may differ sharply as well, due to long-held expectations regarding gender. "Men of few words" and women who speak more openly are common, if far from universal, in family life.

Japan is changing, however, with more women working, more men assuming "maternal" roles, and families taking a wide array of forms. What might happen when a family's breadwinner and domestic roles are reversed, rejected or all absorbed by one person? How might women pursue identities outside the home and men pursue rich communication with family members? What transpires when the domestic circle overlaps with a multigenerational business, also an evolving feature of traditional culture?

The bathroom at our house has two mirrors. One is the usual type that comes with the sink. The other is a super fancy, oval mirror with a wooden frame carved in a floral design. It hangs next to our sink, and I call it the Snow White mirror. Our little bathroom shouldn't need two mirrors, and the Snow White design doesn't exactly fit our lifestyle, given that it's just Dad and me. But really, it's precisely because it's just us two that we have the mirror ...

My dad gets up every day at 6am. With an unshaven face and bedhead, still in his pyjamas, he heads to the kitchen. Ever since I was in preschool, our breakfast has been fried eggs, *natto*,[1] *miso*[2] soup with tofu, and pickled vegetables. As he cracks the eggs and slices the tofu, Dad also starts the washing machine. And he wakes me up:

"Jun. Get up. Up!"

He calls this exactly two times.

Routines are powerful things. When my dad calls me the second time, I really do get right up.

By the time I head to the kitchen hiking up my pyjama pants, breakfast is on the table and the washing machine has started its spin cycle, shaking and clattering.

As Dad reads the newspaper and I watch TV, we eat. We pass the soy sauce and jab our chopsticks into the crock of pickles with precision timing. Our hands manoeuvre around each other, never colliding, like robot hands in a factory. There's no need to speak. At the end I say, "*Gochiso-sama.*"[3]

Then I brush my teeth in the bathroom and change for school. My dad cleans up the kitchen and hangs out the laundry.

"I'm off," I say.

He grunts: "Oh" or "Ah".

After I leave for school, Dad cleans the house, shaves, dresses and heads down to the shop. He's the second-generation owner of a yarn shop. The shop sits on the ground floor, and we live right above.

About the time Dad raises the shutter, Mr Murano arrives by bicycle with his packed lunch. Mr Murano has worked in the shop since my grandfather's time.

---

1 A traditional Japanese dish of fermented soybeans.

2 A fermented soybean paste.

3 Thanks for the meal.

Neither Dad nor Mr Murano act at all like salesmen. When customers arrive, the two men welcome them with "*Irasshaimase!*"[4] And that's it, they go quiet. I have never seen them make small talk or even smile!

How a yarn shop run by two silent men can stay afloat is one of the seven wonders of our shopping district. In fact, it's wonder number one.

It helps that Dad and Mr Murano knit. It's a yarn shop, so they should; but anyway. They're good. Even now, Dad hand-knits all of my sweaters. His stuff is popular even with the girls in my class and their mums: if I wear a new design of his to school, the mums will go to the shop to buy yarn and ask for the pattern. So, I contribute to the bottom line.

From a customer's perspective, I guess our shop offers stylish samples and useful advice; plus, you can look at yarn for ages and no one'll bother you. I suppose that makes for a nice atmosphere. If you can ignore the two geezers knitting in the back.

When I get home from school, if it's not a cram school[5] day, I go buy food for our supper. Usually, I get fried meat cakes or croquettes from the butcher, dried fish from the fish seller or takeout from the ramen place.

Dad closes up shop at 7pm. I help, and depending on how hungry I am, I either eat ahead or wait and eat with him. Just like at breakfast, I end the meal with *Gochiso-sama*.

At nine in the evening, Dad finishes his bath. Then, he stands in front of the Snow White mirror and begins muttering some words. I have never really watched him do this – I've never wanted to watch – but I think he starts with, "Mirror, Mirror, on the wall."

This is his ritual. And with it, he transforms … into my mum. In summer, he's my mum with only boxers on, but anyway …

4 Welcome to the store!
5 Classes conducted by private schools after regular school hours to provide intensive coaching to prepare students for examinations.

"Jun, Honey, did you do your homework?"

"I got a call from your cram school teacher, Jun. She said your math scores are slipping. Don't you think you've been playing video games way too much?"

"So, Akihiro's dad says he'll drop you off at soccer practice on Sunday. I've washed your uniform and put it in the chest of drawers, and your new socks are there too, so be sensible and wear them, OK?"

My mum talks and talks. Whiskers and all.

I used to think that maybe Dad should change into women's clothing for this shtick, to make it less strange, but I'm used to it now.

"OK, what do you want to read today? It's been forever since we read *Two Years' Vacation* by Jules Verne. You love that book! I wish you'd take a few more titles out of the library. When I was your age, Jun, I devoured the Arséne Lupin books."

My whiskered mum always reads to me before I sleep.

Last year, we argued and I finally got her to quit singing me lullabies. But Dad turning into Mum and Mum reading to me never changed. I guess it all serves a purpose.

My real mum – the one without facial hair – left us right after I started preschool. She left my dad and she left me.

Even though she had abandoned us, I missed her. I ached for her. I hated my dad. I had no clue why my mum had left, but I figured it must be my dad's fault that she'd gone. I guess I'd heard the adults' gossip: "I get that he's a man of few words, but there's such a thing as too quiet, right? I mean, I'm his neighbour and never hear his voice!"

The woman who runs the bookshop next door talks about Dad this way, even now.

When Mum left, I cried constantly. I ran off whenever Dad tried to hold me.

My mother was gone. With her gone, I couldn't sleep. Night after night, I buried my head in my blanket and soaked my pillow with tears.

Then, Dad went out and bought the Snow White mirror. And he began pretending to be Mum.

"Now, stop crying. Starting today, I'll be Mum. At night, until you can get to sleep, I'll be Mum, so try and calm down."

With awkward words and an earnest face, Dad became whiskered Mum. Gross! It makes me laugh to think of it now, but at the time, I was boiling mad.

"But you're *Dad*!"

I tried throwing off my covers, but whiskered Mum pinned me down.

"I'm your mum, Honey. I'll be Mum now. Just give me a chance."

And stubbly Mum started singing me a lullaby in a hoarse voice. At least, I think it was a lullaby. I couldn't make out which song it was. It was sad, like weeping, but I still fell asleep.

Each night after that, Dad would stand in front of the Snow White mirror. To transform, he seemed to need the act of muttering his "spell" in that exact spot. The mirror helped.

Gradually, I got used to Dad's ritual. I accepted that he had two personalities. This became so normal that there were certain things I would tell him only when he was in Dad mode, and certain things I would tell him only when he was whiskered Mum. The things Dad couldn't tell me, he too would save for when he was Mum.

"Well, your dad is your dad, isn't he? It can't be helped. But he loves you, Jun, and he wants the best for you, and he wants to protect you and make every day a good day for you. He just has trouble saying that out loud, I think." This, my whiskered mum would say without batting an eye. It was the kind of thing both parent and son might remember later with a blush, but in the moment, since I was so used to it, I'd just nod and say, "Yeah, I know."

The mirror was a prop that Dad and I needed at first, basically. But now, I think I can handle Dad okay without it. He, on the other hand, can't stop pretending to be Mum. He thinks that if he doesn't become Mum, he can't ask me about school and cram school and friends and such. Me, I could just tell him everything while I stir my *natto* or help him close up shop.

"Why should I stop being Mum at bedtime? I look forward to this, too, you know! Now, let's read."

"Come on, seriously!"

"Hush, you. Into bed."

Whiskered Mum has muscles. If I take too long, she can just toss me into bed. Can you imagine an 11-year-old boy who hasn't beaten his mum in wrestling even once? I am that boy.

Lately, I've started teasing a little, though.

"Hey, Mum? Dad still hasn't sold that one sweater he knitted in springtime, has he?"

"Which sweater, Honey?"

"The salmon pink mohair."

"Well, that's a store sample."

"But he sells the samples when the seasons change."

"Salmon pink works fine for fall!"

"What? They change everything to those 'chic' dull fall colours, except that one? It's weird!"

"It's an accent."

Whiskered Mum can be really stubborn.

Even Mr Murano has been shaking his head over the salmon pink mohair. He says that Dad doesn't want to sell that sweater, really. If a customer seems to be checking it out, Dad will rush it to the back. Then, just when it seems he's put it away for good, he'll display it again. Mr Murano thinks he has someone special in mind for it.

"The sleeves on that sweater are different lengths, you know," whiskered Mum finally tells me.

Even I know it is time for some truth now. "Well, the piano teacher at that music store across the street played tennis when she was young," I'd say. "I heard her mention once that when she buys ready-made sweaters, the right sleeve always feels too short."

"Hmm, really?"

"Mm-hmm. I bet Dad heard her say it, too. She always buys navy and grey yarn from us, but I think salmon pink would look great on her."

I go to the trouble of saying all that, and yet whiskered Mum still changes the subject.

"Well. How about *Robinson Crusoe* tonight?"

I guess we'll need the Snow White mirror a bit longer, until my dad can just open up as Dad.

Author's Note

I originally wrote "Mirror, Mirror" as part of a series of stories with folktale motifs for *Onigashima Tsūshin*, a journal that I put together with several other authors in Japan. "Mirror, Mirror" was later published in the short story collection *Miracle Family*.

Daily life in a father-son family, even if it appears barren, will overflow with small expressions of affection. How might a father and son who rarely speak, nonetheless understand one another? I also wanted to write about a woman who needs to have feelings put into words.

Some parents and children can communicate without words, but there are those like the absent mother in "Mirror, Mirror" who do need them. To create the happy families we all desire, I think we can put in effort to observe those around us and do what supports them.

I write my stories with pleasure, and when I finish writing a story, I think, *Ah, that was fun*. I truly enjoy writing. I will be content if readers of this story come to the end and say, "Ah, that was fun!"

Translator's Note

I enjoy translating fiction that opens a window on Japan while exploring universal themes, such as loving a parental figure despite – or perhaps because of – that person's quirks. The son in "Mirror, Mirror" by Sachiko Kashiwaba adores a father who feels he can only converse with his son when in the guise of a woman.

How was this challenging to translate? Well, the Japanese language features distinct male and female speech patterns that English lacks, so I had to puzzle out different ways to make the father sound male at times, and female at other times. Two tools I used only when he was speaking as Mum were italics for emphasis and a pet name for Jun: Honey.

A key technique for translating dialogue (conversation in literature) is reading it aloud again and again, in both the original and the translation, to see if characters "sound like themselves" in the new language. Acting and moving around like the characters helps, too!

By the way, check out how the main characters in "Mirror, Mirror" read fiction in translation (from English and French) – as you have just done – and organise parts of their lives around a German fairy tale. Discovering how stories travel across borders, into people's lives and even into new stories is one of the great delights of being a translator!

La Rangku – The Kite Prince

Niduparas Erlang
Translated by Annie Tucker

First published in Indonesian in *Sindo*, 28 February 2010.

In 1997, a German researcher, Wolfgang Bieck, postulated that Kaghati was the first and oldest kite in the world and was at least 4,000 years old. His research was based on the discovery of ancient paintings on the walls of the Sugi Patani cave in Liangkobori Village in Muna, South Sulawesi. Each Indonesian region has its own kite with distinctive form and function, for example, to celebrate the rice harvest, repel pests or to ask the gods for protection.

While most kites are made from fabric or paper, Kaghati was made from yam leaf. Its measurements were based on its maker: the length was based on the maker's height, measured from the bottom of his feet to his fingertips with his arms reaching up to the sky, and the width was based on his arm span, measured from the tip of his right middle finger to the left with his arms outstretched. Kaghati also had a tail made from *lontar*[1] or *enau*[2] leaves that made a shrill humming sound when the kite was flown.

In 2013, the Kaghati was designated as Intangible Cultural Heritage by the Indonesian Ministry of Education and Culture. In August 2014, Southeast Sulawesi hosted the International Kite Festival, with international participants from Holland, France, Australia, Sweden, Singapore and the USA.

The kite that Wadi was flying climbed higher and higher as he let out the string. It seemed to get smaller and smaller, until all

---

1   A tall fan palm of Africa, India and Malaysia.
2   A medium-sized palm native to tropical Asia, mainly Malaysia and Indonesia.

that was left of it was a four-cornered speck floating under a blue dry-season sky, weaving between clouds that were gathering and marching north. Neither its ribboned tail nor its wings could be seen by the naked eye; only its string, the near end of which was tied to an empty condensed milk can, was visible sloping down to earth. Its far point seemed to pierce the air, stripping away the clouds but Wadi, the boy letting out his waxed string until there was none left, knew that the other end was still tied to the tail of the kite as it swayed, blown by the wind.

From the large grin on his face, it was clear Wadi was quite proud of himself for getting his kite to fly so high. He broke out in a dance atop the embankment. He stretched out both of his small arms, then glided along like the aeroplane that had passed over his village once or twice. Sometimes he walked slowly, wobbling as if his body was off-balance or maybe he was imagining himself as a circus acrobat crossing a tightrope, but Wadi didn't fall. He stopped for a moment, gazing upwards towards the kite, which was about to take a nosedive. His left hand tightly grasped the condensed milk can bobbin, while his right hand pulled-released-pulled the thread so that the kite didn't come tumbling down.

"Mother!" he suddenly shouted. "Come back down to earth! Climb onto my kite and ride it down. Come down … come down …" His shouts resounded shrilly, parting the clouds, gnawing at the afternoon sky. But they weren't enough to rouse the heavens, which had taken his mother and wouldn't let her go.

Every time he asked where his mother was, or whenever he had a fever and cried out for her in a delirium, Father would tell him, with a smile that seemed a bit forced – maybe because it was masking his pain – that his mother now made her home in heaven.

"Why does Mother make her home in heaven, Father? Why doesn't she just live here with us?" Wadi asked one night, sniffling.

And so Father began to tell him about heaven – about its flower garden, about the grand houses by which flowed a river of honey, a river of milk and a river of spring water, about all the eases and pleasures, about all the furnishings and trappings there that were available for free. Everything he described seemed so enchanting.

"Well then, why doesn't Mother invite us there?" he complained.

"Mother won't invite us, Child. But one day, when we are called, we will go there to keep her company …"

"But where is heaven, Father?"

"Way up on high. Above the clouds, above the stars," Father said, looking up and pointing at the stars glimmering on the other side of the window pane.

Wadi looked upwards, too. His eyes, clear but still swollen from crying, followed Father's finger, pointing on a rising slant, ascending towards the night sky. And in the dark sky, looking towards the glimmering constellations, some of which were in the shape of a kite, Wadi tried to imagine his mother. She had been an elegant young woman whose wavy hair hung in loose curls down her back or, at least, that was how she looked in the portrait Wadi had seen. In that portrait she had been smiling, sweet like milk. And her cheeks had been ripe and blushing, orange like a mango. But that image had been replaced by all the young women in his village who would invite him to play, or with the neighbourhood women, some of whom were widows and who were maybe interested in Father.

When he fell asleep, Wadi dreamt he had wings and his Father also had wings, and together they flew up to Mother's house in heaven. They lived happily there, with all the enchanting furnishings and trappings they could use for free. And the next day when he awoke, Wadi began to practice flapping his two arms like a baby bird, running and gliding. The only problem was, he couldn't figure out how to fly. Father said arms weren't wings. Wadi nodded even though he didn't understand, still secretly holding on to the dream that his arms would turn into wings and fly him up to Mother's dwelling.

But then that dream came crashing down, along with the cracking branches and breaking twigs of a rose apple tree, which he and his playmate Mamad had been climbing. From his perch, all Wadi could do was watch fearfully and tremble as Mamad went bouncing and crashing down through the branches, and then landing on the dry, pebble-strewn earth with a thud. In the end, it wasn't just Mamad's right arm that was smashed and broken so badly that it had to be amputated, Wadi's dreams were also smashed, and had to be amputated, too.

* * *

"Dad, tell me about kites," he asked after the previous year's harvest. Usually every year after the harvest, a kite festival was held in the village. It wasn't a bustling provincial or national kite festival, it was just a small and simple affair held to show gratitude for a harvest that usually wasn't even all that abundant. The festival was held by and for the local villagers, and the rules were quite simple, too. There was no jury to evaluate the beauty of the kites' shapes, their resilience in the wind, their sonorous hum or buzz as they flew, or other qualities – the winning kite was simply the one able to stay up in the air the longest without breaking or taking a nosedive. But Wadi, unlike most of the wheedling village children, didn't want his father to make a kite for him, he had simply asked his father to tell him about kites.

So Father told him about the very first kite, about Kaghati from Muna in Southeast Sulawesi; about a king named La Pasindaedaeno who sacrificed his child, La Rangku, and how yams then grew on the prince's grave; about a kite, Kaghati, made from one of those yam leaves with a pineapple fibre thread, which was flown for seven days and seven nights, until its string was cut on the last night; about the Muna people's belief that Kaghati would fly all the way until it reached the sun and bestow blessings upon them.

After that, Wadi had a new dream of becoming La Rangku. He dreamt of becoming a kite and flying to the sun but Wadi didn't really want to fly to the sun, he wanted to fly to heaven, where his mother was. He wanted to fly with Father, to go find Mother, to answer the call, to live happily in a grand house on the banks of a river of honey, a river of milk and a river of spring water. "Aren't both the sun and heaven above the clouds and stars?" he thought. So Wadi asked for a kite ...

* * *

Tonight, I have found a quiet that seems to cling wistfully to your back. Maybe the cold, the kind of cold that only comes on rain-drenched nights like tonight, brings that quiet with it. A heavy rain has made all the stones slippery, the earth muddy, left the tent drenched and leaking, and has swiftly extinguished the flames of our bonfire and the flames in my worried heart. In my mounting anxiety, we took shelter in vain, because with all this rain my clothes are still getting wet, and yours probably are, too. The cold, rustling wind is shaking the leaves loose, knocking over huts. And the thundering of the waterfall is getting louder.

To warm your body, as the rain abates, you decide to cook some noodles inside the drenched and leaking tent. The camping stove flame is blue, but its warmth doesn't reach my skin, my heart. With my dampness, the cold penetrates to my ribs. I am still shivering, still worried. But you don't pay me any mind.

After wordlessly taking water from the spring, you quickly heat the water and cook a few packets of noodles. For some reason, I almost start to enjoy the scene – recording every movement of your body, relishing my shivers, taking heed of the quiet that is hardening over your back, and savouring the glimpses I get of the curve of your cheek, the slant of your eyelids when you look over at me. "Look at me, out of the corner of your perfect eyes. And I will enter your world, in secret …"[3] Like my kite, which secretly flew to heaven.

And secretly you slip away, too; at three in the morning, I find you near the waterfall, which spills countless litres of water every minute from about 20 metres above us. Maybe all the tears I have shed thinking of my mother would be as voluminous – I don't know. But the air and atmosphere here is as it was before. Still. Damp. Chilling. Restless. The only noise comes from the chirping crickets and the pounding of Curug Gumawang Waterfall in the creeping darkness.

Silent and cold, under the dim light of the moon, we are still a full spear's length apart from one another, still not talking. We are as frozen and mute as statues – although not perfect statues, because we still occasionally shiver and tremble. And maybe this is my way of revelling in every scene that we are playing out tonight – without much dialogue, without many gestures, I enjoy them in silence, in a silent secrecy. And maybe there is still love between us, but it seems that language is not enough to express it and can no longer be trusted, so silence becomes the safest choice.

And anyway, although I hope it is not true, I have begun to suspect that love is like a brightly coloured cork that grabs your attention, floating on the dense and murky water of the vessel that I call the heart. Our love – it could be mine, it could be

---

3   Adapted from a poem by Indonesian poet FR Herwan, titled "Memandangmu di Balik Permainan".

Mother's, it could be yours – for someone or something is a cork, and that cork keeps floating and dancing just as it pleases. Its colour grows more alluring and brighter with each meeting, as the intense feelings of togetherness build. Oh, how that cork blazes, with cascades of light that radiate out in all directions and dances the most beautiful dance.

But without warning, the mighty and invisible hand of the rain comes to pound the vessel, making ripples that swell in expanding circles to become waves. The thick opaque water, that was so calm at first, is shaken. Some of it rebounds off the cork, splashing and evaporating into the ether, or maybe disintegrating as it seeps into the barren land.

I look at the landscape, letting conversation fall away. You look at the landscape, letting conversation fall away. But maybe also in secret, without me knowing, you are knitting dreams from a spider web. Like the dreams I once knit from the fibres of a pineapple leaf.

Ah, in truth I want to invite you to talk, or to go tiptoeing, go swimming, fly kites, learn how to fly. But this rain disconcerts me, it makes me uneasy and reminds me of the kite that I once flew so expertly, 14 years ago. Is this the night that Mother will come and find me? Or maybe tonight my kite will be conquered by the weather? Collapsed, broken and torn apart. Oh ... truly, every time the rain beats down, I become *La Rangku*, the Kite Prince, scorched by the sun.

"I'm a daughter. I'm not allowed to fly kites." Your words suddenly break the leaden silence of the night. But it is as if you aren't addressing anyone, just talking to yourself.

Still I want to propose: "Don't you want to fly kites with me? Come, and we will wait for my Mother to give us her blessing."

But the words catch in my throat.

Translator's Note

I was drawn to translate the short stories of Niduparas Erlang because of the evocative and distinctive way he captures different local traditions in his work, from the perspective of compelling and identifiable characters. We first met (virtually) through our mutual participation in APSAS (Apresiasi Sastra, or Literature Appreciation), a group formed to promote and support Indonesian literature in translation. His work stood out to me with its striking imagery and the way his narrative was crafted. While some of the scenarios or environments in his work were unfamiliar to me, since Indonesia is a vast archipelago home to so many different peoples with distinct languages and life worlds, his stories always got me to feel something. For example, "*La Rangku*" taught me about the kite legend, but it also struck me with its air of melancholy mystery, which seemed to so aptly capture feelings of loss and the challenges of human connection.

One puzzle for a translator of his stories, including this one, is that, as mentioned, Indonesia has so many local languages and dialects, each steeped in its own rich cultural context; this means that some words are not easily "translatable." I want to avoid adding in too many wordy explanations that would distract from the narrative flow, and yet I also don't want readers to be confused. In these circumstances, I like to leave an original word or two, with the translation immediately following, such as you see in the title of this story: "*La Rangku* – The Kite Prince".

Finding Subi

Janani Janarthanan

Family systems in India are undergoing a change. While some remain in larger family structures in their native villages, many individuals now break into nuclear family units and migrate to the closest cities in search of better educational and financial opportunities. Villages that are cut off from the prospects of urbanisation are most affected by city-bound migration, transforming them into a vestige of the past, into small pockets of nostalgia that are re-visited when time permits.

In an attempt to maintain their cultural roots and identity despite the changes in their surroundings, individuals often return with their families to their villages annually to celebrate festivities and temple anniversaries. Such traditions also help the generations raised outside the ambit of their villages to learn, experience and understand first-hand the origins of their cultural identity.

During such occasions, these villages reunite their diaspora, becoming points of cultural rendezvous between those who have moved out and those who remained.

All of it looked exactly the same. Nothing had changed. Not the smooth tarred highway roads leading to their little village, not the rows and acres of paddy fields that flanked the roads, not even the coconut trees which seemed to spring out of the ground abruptly. Looking outside the car window, Anu loudly tried to put together the letters on signboards, shop banners and posters, all scrawled in her mother tongue, Tamil.

"*Appa*![1] How much longer?" she whined, pulling away from her mother who was braiding her hair into pigtails. Sitting on her mother's lap in the shotgun seat, Anu could not wait to reach their destination.

---

1 Father in Tamil, Kannada and other South Indian languages.

"Anu! Stop moving. Sit straight!" her mother scolded.

"*Appa*, go faster! Subi will be waiting," Anu stressed, slapping the car's dashboard.

"That's alright. And I don't want you two gallivanting around the village as soon as we get there," her mother added, tying the elastic band at the end of Anu's long hair.

Her mother's words were a little too late. Anu had already charted out a mental itinerary of all the things she and Subi would do on their three-day weekend. It would include, and not be limited to, skipping stones at the village stream, dipping their feet in it and getting tickled by the little fish that ate away at the dirt, jumping terraces and teasing Bujji, the lame black cat in the village.

There was a bond between Subi and Anu that many families would envy. But that was it – Subi and Anu were not family.

Subi was the granddaughter of their cook, Kamalamma, in the village. Kamalamma was a fragile old lady with stringy hair and soft, wrinkly skin. She became Subi's sole guardian after her parents died in a tragic accident when Subi was just a toddler. Anu, on the contrary, lived in the big city which was 350 kilometres away and had a big family. She was the tallest girl in the fourth grade but she was shorter than Subi. However, nobody could tell the difference just by looking at them. Anu had bushy hair that always bounced a few centimetres above her scalp. Subi, on the other hand, had straight long hair that had to be braided and secured with a ribbon. She had a gap between her two front teeth, which Anu's mother said would need braces when she grew older. Every year, the two girls would meet over the summer when it was time for the village temple's annual festival. Anu's father, like all those who had grown up in the village, came back every year with his family.

As soon as they drove down the cobbled path of their street, the familiar sight of houses sandwiched together, with tightly packed red roof tiles, emerged into view. The sun bore through the body of their car and sweat coated their necks as they parked outside their ancestral home. Over the years, the house had been bleached into a dull yellow. It bore wounds of old age which exposed its brick and cement flesh in patches. The window shutters, which had been painted a shade of blue, now withered and peeled away with touch. The occupants of the big yellow house seldom cared to notice the dilapidated exterior during their annual trips. It was a long rectangular house with high ceilings and fans that extended from the roof with long necks. If all the doors were open, one could see the padlocked door of the backyard from the foot of the veranda. This straight stretch often served as the racing track for Anu and Subi's races.

As soon as the car came to a halt, Anu tore into a sprint, running into the big yellow house. Stopping at the dimly lit kitchen, Anu saw old Kamalamma wearing a cotton sari with her stringy hair collected in a sparse bun. She was bending over a pot of boiling milk at the stove; cooking on the burner next to it was a huge *kadai*[2] of *upma*,[3] the evening *tiffin*[4] for the family.

"Anu, *Kutty*![5] When did you arrive, where is your father and mother?" Kamalamma crackled to life on seeing the little girl standing just outside the kitchen.

"Where is Subi, *Paati*?"[6]

"School should be over, she'll be coming home anytime now. Come here, let me look at you ... you've grown so tall, *Kutty* ..."

---

2 An Indian wok.
3 A dish made from vermicelli/dry-roasted semolina/coarse rice flour mixed with chopped vegetables, common in South India.
4 A light tea-time meal.
5 A term of endearment for young children in the states of Tamil Nadu and Kerala.
6 Grandmother in Tamil.

"Okay," Anu responded, sprinting away before Kamalamma could get hold of her, lest she should be forced to eat *upma* or worse, drink a glass of milk.

Around the time Anu and her family had parked outside their house in the village, the school bell outside Subi's classroom rang. Subi had been counting the minutes to the end of the school day since it began that morning. She was looking forward to the long weekend and all that she had to tell Anu. She would tell her everything – from how she got the scrape on her knee climbing a tree to her new headmistress, the noisy boys in her class who pulled her hair and everything she could think of. As Subi ran home from school, a familiar voice pierced through the air from the other end of the street.

"Hey, Subi! Are you still as slow as you were last year?" Anu called out.

* * *

On the day of the temple festival, the speaker outside Anu's house blared morning prayers as early as 6am, but the entire street was already awake. Overnight, many of the houses had been adorned with decorative lights and in the streets closer to the temple, electric poles held speakers every few hundred metres. By the morning of the festival, the entire street was lined with cars, resembling a mall parking lot.

About an hour later, after being chided for dozing off in the bathroom, a sleep-deprived Anu sat in front of two fluffy *idlis*[7] laid on a plantain leaf. Next to her, Subi was almost done with her meal. Anu eyed Subi's simple everyday *kurta*[8] and pants enviously as her own starchy golden *lehenga*[9] nibbled at her waist.

---

7 A popular South Indian breakfast dish made by steaming a batter of fermented black lentils and rice.

8 A loose, collarless shirt or blouse worn in South India.

9 A full ankle-length skirt worn by young girls and women in India.

"Come on! How long are you going to take to finish that, slowpoke?" Subi asked.

"Faster than you," Anu replied, hurriedly stuffing the contents of her plate into her mouth and washing it all down with a glass of water.

"*Paati* says you'll throw up if you eat like that," Subi retorted.

Anu pretended to throw up and Subi burst into laughter.

"Anu! Behave yourself! Or the both of you will get it from me. Is this how you are going to behave all day? Sit straight … Now, the temple is going to be crowded with lots of people today and I want you both to be on your best behaviour. No running around the place. No talking to strangers or going with them. And always stay together! Do you understand?" Anu's mother barked.

The girls nodded in unison.

"Now, finish up and sit in the veranda, we'll be leaving soon."

Both girls, still giggling, made a beeline for the veranda. A bustle had manifested in every room in the big yellow house. Anu's relatives had steadily arrived over the last two days to attend the temple festivities. She didn't like her relatives, much less any of her cousins; they were either too old or too young for her.

At 10am, a horde of descendants of the big yellow house pushed themselves out of its doors, decked in fine clothes and shimmering silk sarees. The men wore crisp white shirts that stuck to their skin with perspiration and *dhoti*[10] that stiffly held on owing to the starch they had consumed. The sarees were beginning to stick to the bodies of the women and their sweat matted stray wisps of black hair to their foreheads. The air was a strange concoction of lilies and body odour. As they walked to the temple, the back opening of their blouses showed early signs of heat rash developing and droplets of sweat occasionally dripped over them.

---

10 A lower garment worn by men in India consisting of a piece of cloth that is wrapped around the waist and secured with a knot.

What truly stood out about the village's temple festival was the number of people who enthusiastically thronged the event, year after year. The village heads would collaborate with the temple authorities and organise the festivities with elaborate pomp and show. They would begin collecting funds six months ahead and plan every detail from the concerts to the free meals. One temple would host and feed hundreds of mouths and one village deity would grant hundreds of wishes throughout the day.

Unlike the others, Anu and Subi felt equal parts of joy and dread about the village festival. Joy because they anticipated an entire day of fun and good food, and dread because of the loud music that would peak with the rising devotion. When that happened, the temple bells would come together in a loud clamour to the percussion of small cymbals. Drums and horns would blare in loud competition to deafening decibels and infants would often burst into tears.

As the colourful ceremony neared its end that day, all the devotees huddled together in prayer as the *aarti*[11] was performed. The bells and the prayers got louder. Everyone had their palms clasped together, their heads bent and eyes closed. An uneasy feeling arose in the pit of Subi's stomach as the music became louder. She shut her eyes tightly and grabbed Anu's hand. Anu squeezed her hand back. As they waited for the ceremony to finish, their heartbeats rose to the loud music that was steadily picking up in volume.

That was when they heard it. A sudden murmur of confusion began and fingers were being pointed in the direction of the voices. It was a heavy woman in a purple saree with white streaks in her hair standing towards their left. Suddenly, the woman began shaking and her eyes bulged out. Someone around them let out a scream but Anu and Subi were too stupefied to open their mouths.

---

11 A Hindu temple ritual that is performed towards the end of a ceremony or prayer.

Their frozen eyes watched it unfold. Men in the woman's vicinity inched closer to help her. Anu and Subi were pushed aside. A sudden commotion erupted and the people standing behind them started pushing forward, trying to get a better view.

As the music rose, the woman who was now supported by a few men collapsed to the ground. The music at the temple grew deafeningly loud and so did the commotion around them. Anu felt squashed and breathless. She wanted to get out immediately and she released Subi's hand. As more people pushed forward to see the action, Anu retreated into the crowd and into herself.

A few moments later, the woman in the purple saree had regained consciousness and the crowd began dispersing. That was when Anu's mother realised that her daughter was not standing by her side.

"Anu?" Her mother called out, frantically looking around for her daughter.

"Anu? Anu!" She cried again, this time wading through the crowd.

The voice of Anu's mother had lost its usual command. An unknown fear made her hands cold and her lips quiver.

"She's here!" A voice called out behind her.

A crying Anu was found with tears streaming down her cheeks in the middle of the crowd. Her mother rushed to her side and smothered her with kisses, but Anu did not snap out of it until later that afternoon when she returned home. The image of the woman in the purple saree haunted her. Anu and her mother did not realise until later that day that Subi, too, had disappeared in the crowd.

* * *

As she beheld the sight of the woman in the purple saree, Subi's eyes refused to blink. It seemed like people were pushing from all sides and with one quick tug, Subi lost Anu's hand. She felt squeezed and shoved as more people edged closer to get a glimpse of the woman. She found herself tossed around, separated from Anu and her golden dress. She frantically looked around for familiar faces but the ones that met her eyes didn't seem familiar. Confused and disoriented in a sea of people, Subi looked around unable to suppress the dread that was rising in her stomach.

"Anu?" Subi cried out, her voice choked with tears. Unable to see Anu or her mother, Subi felt scared and alone for the first time. She found herself jostled and bumped around even more, as people seemed to gather together in a frenzy like bees. Everywhere she looked, she was met with the waists and chests of people, brushing against their clothes and scraping by their silks. The bells and voices grew louder and louder around her. Unable to resist the wave, Subi stood distraught and utterly lost. She ran about trying to find Anu. She looked up at everyone that passed her, but no one seemed to notice her. For nobody would notice a girl in cheap pants and *kurta*.

Until someone did. Subi heard a gruff voice behind her, "Hey … are you alone?"

* * *

Elsewhere, a frightened Anu snuggled up against her mother's shoulder. Caressed and carried around, she slowly began to reel out of her fright. When they reached home, Kamalamma was instructed to give her a little something to drink. Kamalamma did as she was told. Handing over a glass of milk to the girl, she asked her where Subi was.

Subi?

Anu's fear was completely washed away and replaced with guilt. It was then that she realised she had let go of Subi's hand.

* * *

The man knelt down in front of Subi and asked her again, "Child, where are your parents?"

Subi could see that he was a tall, strong man. He was wearing a red shirt, khaki pants and a brown belt between the two. Around his belt hung a black walkie-talkie, alive with chatter paused only by empty static.

Subi's tears choked her.

"Can you not find the people you came with?" he enquired again.

Subi managed to shake her head, sniffling loudly.

"It's okay. We'll find your parents now. I'll help you find them. Come with me."

Subi wiped her tears but stood still, snivelling in the same spot.

"It's alright, you can come with me. I'm a policeman. Here look, this is a special police walkie-talkie." He added with a smile, "You can hold it if you want."

Subi knew who the police were. She knew that much, from movies and the old glossy picture books in school. Just then, the walkie-talkie crackled to life with words Subi couldn't catch. The policeman held Subi's hand and they walked towards the station tent outside the temple.

"Do you want to eat something?" the young policeman asked her.

"No, I'm not hungry … thank you, Sir," Subi replied, adding the last part in English as an afterthought.

The young policeman smiled at her. "Which standard are you studying?"

"Fourth standard, Periyar Primary School."

"Even I studied there! What's your name?"

"Subi."

"Do you like it at school?"

Subi shook her head.

"Hmph … I don't remember liking it, either," the young policeman replied.

Subi smiled for the first time that afternoon.

"So tell me now, who should we call to come and take you home?"

By the time Anu's mother hesitantly walked into the station tent, all of Subi's blues had flown away. She was giggling uncontrollably when she found out that her maths teacher had always worn his spectacles at the tip of his nose, since the policeman was his student. Subi suddenly hopped off the table she was sitting on and burst out, "That's Anu's mother!"

"Subi? There you are. Thank God!" As relief spread all over Anu's mother's face, she knelt down and hugged the girl. She gave her a little kiss on her forehead. Nobody ever kissed Subi, except *Paati*.

"You gave us such a fright. We've been looking for you all over the temple."

"How are you related to the child, Ma'am?"

"She is our cook's granddaughter."

"And her parents?"

"She lives with us; her parents are not alive."

"Alright, we need you to give your details and then you can take her. Hold young children's hands tightly, and be more careful in the future," the policeman warned. "She was lucky I happened to find her."

"Yes, thank you so very much, Sir. It won't happen again!" Anu's mother replied.

As soon as they entered the house, Kamalamma picked Subi up and gave her a big kiss. It was the second time she was kissed that day.

Behind *Paati*, Anu stood still, unable to meet Subi's eyes.

But Subi smiled. She knew just what to say. "Anu, do you know, I met a policeman today … He had a big moustache but he was not scary at all …"

Anu quietly slipped her hand over Subi's as the latter continued unfazed. But this time, Anu knew better. She interlocked her fingers with Subi's ever so tightly.

Author's Note

Many families like mine often visit their native villages for festivities, making it an annual tradition among the village diaspora. This helps to retain a collective cultural identity and breeds a feeling of belonging in a country where migration to cities increases with every generation.

The story "Finding Subi" is modelled after my experiences in my native village near Gunaseelam, Trichy, Tamil Nadu, and written in a way that introduces and explains the social and cultural setting to those outside my cultural circumference. While the setting and events are modelled after my own personal experiences, the characters in the story are fictitious with no resemblance to anyone living or dead. I imagined societal differences between my principal characters so as to highlight the reality and its relevance to the social fabric in India. Using children for narrative voices and dwelling on their relationship with each other was a deliberate choice as children do not perceive socio-economic differences as strongly as adults do. The children in the story experience feelings of adventure, excitement and guilt simultaneously as they learn of important values like family, friendship and religion. Their treatment of such matters is impulsive and honest, which is often absent in adults who treat such topics with more rationality and social desirability.

In terms of style, the writing aims to replicate a child's point of view, limiting authorial voice. I perceive reading as an act of empathy, where readers allow themselves to be transported to distant lands and feel memories that are not their own. Hence, I have incorporated my own experiences in order to keep it authentic, in the hope that it will resonate even with those outside my cultural sphere.

Mummee Kuah

Asma' Jailani

> Hari Raya Aidilfitri, also known as Eid al-Fitr, is a religious
> holiday celebrated worldwide by Muslims. It marks the end of
> Ramadan, a holy month where Muslims practice the religious
> obligation of fasting from dawn to sunset for the whole month.
> In Malaysia, it is customary for Muslims to seek forgiveness from
> others on the day of Eid, as a way of strengthening bonds and
> letting bygones be bygones. Naturally, it is a joyous occasion that
> brings people together, as it is also customary to visit the homes
> of friends and family to celebrate. Like any other traditional
> holiday, much of the excitement revolves around food. On the
> night before Eid, many families busy themselves with cleaning
> up their houses and preparing a feast for the guests who will visit
> the next day after the Eid prayers.

"How's *Abah*?"[1]

"Same as always. He eats, sleeps, watches TV."

"Does he talk to you?"

"He grunts a little whenever I ask him anything. At this point,
I think that's as good as it's gonna get."

Alya sighs. "Don't say that, Dina. It'll just … take some time."

"It's been a *year, Kakak*."[2]

"He's hurting."

"And we're not?" Irdina's voice is as brittle as it is cutting. A
shaky sigh follows, strained and tinny over the phone. "Sorry, it's
not your fault. I just …"

"I know." Alya understands. Really, she does.

"Not a day goes by where I don't miss her," Irdina says in a
quiet voice.

---

1 Father in Malay.
2 Sister in Malay.

Alya wishes she could cross the kilometres between them to hug her tight. "Me too, Dina. I miss her all the time, too."

There's a beat of silence, a gap filled by their mutual heartbreak.

Alya gathers herself. "I know it's hard Dina, to see *Abah* like that, but we just have to be … patient."

"Yeah." The bitter edge is still there in Irdina's voice, but it's softened somewhat. "Yeah, I know. Anyway, how did the job interview go?"

"I think it went well. But we'll see if they call me back."

"Hm." Irdina makes a non-committal sound, like she doesn't know how to feel about it.

Alya doesn't either, to be fair. A high-paying job at an established law firm in Singapore. It doesn't get much better than that, especially for the likes of an early 20-something who is just starting out in the field. And yet …

"Come back already, will you?" Irdina says. "It's bad enough that *Abang*[3] doesn't even stay in KL anymore."

"It's just two more days. You'll be alright."

"But I'm lonely."

Alya huffs a fond laugh. "You have Mok and *Abah* to keep you company."

"Ah yes, one *chonky*[4] cat and a man who's practically glued to his armchair 24/7. I can just imagine the *sparkling conversations* we'll have."

"That's the spirit."

Irdina scoffs. "I gotta go make dinner, talk to you later, *Kakak*. Bye."

"Bye."

Alya sags into her older brother's worn-out couch as the call ends. Outside, the sky is tinged orange, not quite sunset yet but getting there.

---

3 Brother in Malay.
4 Slang for "chunky" or overweight.

The couch dips as a heavy weight settles into the other end.

"I didn't even hear you come back," Alya says.

Her brother shrugs back at her. "You were pretty engrossed in your conversation with Dina," he says, as Alya shifts over to make room for him. "How was the job interview?"

"It went pretty well, actually. I think I have a good shot."

"Yeah? That's great!"

But in a heartbeat, his expression goes from joy to concern.

"You don't look very excited," he observes. "Or relieved."

"I am!" Alya doesn't know what to do with her hands, so she opts to grab a stray cushion to hug. "I am, but ..."

"But?"

"Well, let's say the firm does accept me ..."

"Which they will."

"I'm glad you have so much faith in me, but listen for a sec. Say they accept me. Then, logically, I'd have to move to Singapore for the job, right?"

"Right," Hakim nods, looking like he's still trying to grasp what she is getting at.

"That would mean leaving Dina alone to take care of *Abah*."

Hakim's brow furrows as the reality hits. "Dina's a responsible kid," he says. "She'll be alright." But even he doesn't look convinced at his own words.

"I can't do that to her, Kim." Alya hugs the cushion tighter to her chest. "It wouldn't be fair."

There is silence as her brother slumps against the cushions, deep in thought. "That's real honourable of you, Alya," he says, finally. "But I think you should give this a little more thought. You've been dreaming of something like this for so long, after all."

"I mean, yeah, but ..."

Alya doesn't bother finishing her sentence. She doesn't need to. They both know what's been left unsaid.

Before, she would have been over the moon about acing her job interview, ecstatic over the possibility of learning from top lawyers at such a prestigious law firm.

But then Mama passed away. And Alya's father was never the same after that.

* * *

The next day finds Alya and Hakim at their aunt's house. She'd invited them over to *buka puasa*[5] with her family.

Before the actual dinner, Muslim families break their day-long fast once it's time for the *maghrib* prayer,[6] with a few dates and some water. They perform their prayers together, and only then do they dine.

Dinners with Alya's relatives are always a grand affair. Known for her culinary prowess, her aunt never fails to go all out, dishing out dish after sumptuous dish. Prawns laden with spicy *sambal*,[7] stingray in steaming bowls of *asam pedas*,[8] an assortment of stir-fried vegetables and more fill the table as they all crowd around to dig in.

Sometime after dinner, after everyone has eaten and the dirty dishes have been dealt with, Alya finds her cousins convening in the middle of the living room.

Her cousin, Salamah, beckons her over. "Check this out," she says. "We were clearing out some stuff earlier today and found this box full of old books and photo albums." Alya plonks herself onto the carpet to join them. She picks up an album to flip through the pages, flicking through faded snapshots of days gone by.

---

5 To break the day's fasting.
6 The sunset prayer, one of the five mandatory daily prayers for Muslims.
7 A spice paste made with chillies, garlic, shallots and other ingredients.
8 A sour and spicy stewed dish.

Among them are pictures of her aunt and her mother in their youth. Her mother in tears as a toddler, mucus dripping from her nose. Her mother and Aunty Sham as young girls, clinging to the back of their father's legs as they grinned at the camera with matching toothy grins. Another where they're seated on a wooden swing, this time as beautiful young women in their prime. Alya pauses as she catches sight of another picture.

It's a picture of her parents on their wedding day. Her mother is beaming at the camera, looking resplendent in a simple white dress with lace trimming. Alya's father, however, dressed in a white *baju melayu*[9] and matching *sampin*,[10] isn't looking at the camera. Instead, he's turned towards her mother, a small smile on his face. Although his smile is slight, it's there regardless, clear as day, reflecting an unbearable fondness. Like he couldn't look away from her, even if he tried. The sight of it evokes in Alya's heart a pang of something bittersweet.

What she would give to see both of their smiles again.

"That takes me back," a voice says. Alya looks up as her aunt settles beside her on the carpet. "Wasn't my sister pretty?"

"Very," Alya agrees with a smile, passing the photo album to her. Her aunt looks over the photograph with warm nostalgia.

"How are things at home?" She asks, flipping over to the next page.

"Same as always," Alya says. "Dina says she's lonely since I've been away, though." She doesn't bother going into details, since her cousins are still around. But Aunty Sham would get it. She knows about Alya's father after all, being the first of their relatives to offer her support after Alya's mother passed on.

"I see." A wan smile crosses her aunt's face. She sets down the

---

9 Traditional clothing worn by Malay men.
10 An embroidered cloth that is wrapped around the waist and usually worn together with *baju melayu* or other traditional clothing.

album in favour of a hardcover notebook, loose papers bursting between its pages. Her face is thoughtful.

A year ago, on the day before Hari Raya Aidilfitri, Alya had sat by her mother's bedside as she held her mother's frail hand between her shaking palms. Dina had sat beside her, shedding silent tears as she held onto their mother's other hand. Behind the two sisters stood Hakim, silent and grave as he rested a hand on each of their shoulders. His mouth was a grim line.

Their father had sat on the bed, right by their mother's side. A single hand stroked their mother's hair back gently; one last tender touch as a parting gift. They didn't want to acknowledge it, but deep down, they knew that this was goodbye.

Alya's mother had been sick for a while. But the illness that had taken root in her was one that was without symptoms in its early stages, leaving them unaware of the sickness festering beneath her skin. By the time they realised what was happening, it was too late. Despite the constant treatment and care, nothing seemed to work. Surgery wasn't an option, due to the extensive spread of the disease within her mother's body over time.

There were periods of time when she seemed to get better, only to relapse weeks later. Eventually, the period of weeks turned into days. Regular doctor visits turned into an extended hospital stay.

Finally, when things seemed most bleak and the prognosis was far from favourable, Alya's mother made the arrangements to move out of the hospital and back home. She'd decided: if she was facing her final days, then she'd spend them in a place of love, rather than within cold hospital walls.

While everyone else prepared to celebrate Hari Raya Aidilfitri and commemorate the previous month of abstinence and heightened piety, Alya watched the rise and fall of her mother's chest as she took each shallow breath. Instead of spending the night sweeping floors and hanging decorations for the next day's festivities, Alya listened to her mother rasp the *shahadah*[11] one final time, a contented smile on her face as she declared her faith to her Creator once more.

And then she was gone. Here one second and gone the next, like she had simply slipped into a peaceful slumber. If there were silver linings to be found, then it would be the fact that her mother had passed away within the most holy month of the year, something that many Muslims fervently hope and pray will happen to themselves once it is their time to go.

But there was no place for silver linings amidst fresh grief. Not as the sound of her sister's sobbing echoed around the room nor as Alya's own tears which finally spilled down her cheeks. Not as her brother's hand trembled where it rested on her shoulder. Not as her father continued to stroke their mother's hair back, like the motion would ease her journey into the faraway place souls drifted off to after leaving their bodies.

Needless to say, they didn't celebrate Raya that year.

A year later, and the grief is still there. Alya doesn't think it will ever leave. She doesn't expect it to. But at the very least, the pain of her mother's passing was no longer a gaping, ugly wound, stinging from a mere brush of air. It was still there, occupying the space that it had carved out in the cavity of her chest in the early days of her pain, when even breathing felt like too much and her heart constantly frayed, ripping into two. But now it simply settled, leaving a dull ache that made itself known during the bad days. Alya is still getting used to that feeling. But then again, she has plenty of time. The thing that people don't tell you about pain is that you never stop carrying it around with you. You simply get used to it.

---

11 The Muslim declaration of faith and one of the Five Pillars of Islam.

"Oh," her aunt says as she flips through the notebook. "It's my old recipe book! I was wondering where I had put it." Then, she frowns. "It's been damaged by water, though."

"Oh no, how bad is it?" Alya asks.

"A good half of the recipes are ruined," her aunt laments. "What a shame." She perks up the slightest bit, flashing Alya a triumphant look. "Thankfully, I have them all up here," she says, tapping her forehead. "Recipes from my mother, recipes from my mother's mother, and even …"

She flips through the recipe book and stops at a page. The page is filled with cursive writing, in a penmanship that almost seems … familiar. The writing fades off halfway down the page, the rest reduced to blooms of water-damaged ink across the paper.

"This is your mum's *mee kuah*[12] recipe," Aunty Sham says. "Or at least, what's left of it."

Alya turns to her aunt, jaw dropping. "Really?"

"Really." Her aunt grins, passing the book to her. Alya presses her fingers to the familiar scrawl almost reverently.

For as long as she can remember, she's associated Hari Raya with several things: Raya prayers and rushing to the mosque; taking turns with her siblings to kiss their parents' hands, asking for forgiveness for any previous misdoings; greeting all her relatives who came to visit (and maybe solicit a money packet or two from particularly generous aunties and uncles); and of course, *mee kuah*.

Sure, there were the Raya classics to look forward to, like spicy beef *rendang*[13] or sticky rice *pulut*[14] and all manner of cookies and *kuih*[15] to look forward to. But there was nothing quite like her

---

12 A popular noodle soup made with shrimp and beef stock.
13 A slow-cooked, spicy meat stew.
14 Glutinous rice.
15 Traditional bite-sized cakes and snacks.

mother's signature dish of noodle soup that really made Raya feel like Raya for Alya.

"But it isn't actually her recipe," her aunt says.

"What do you mean?"

Aunty Sham flashes her a conspiratorial grin. "Let me tell you something, *Sayang*.[16] Your mother's recipe is actually from your father's mother. Apparently, she found out that your grandmother's *mee kuah* was your father's favourite dish. And naturally, *Kakak* asked your grandmother for her recipe. Because it was so good, I asked your mother to pass it to me, too."

"Those were really tasty noodles," Alya agrees, nodding. "Wait, did you say that *mee kuah* was *Abah*'s favourite?"

"You didn't know?"

"Not at all." Alya weighs this new piece of information in her mind. Her father wasn't really a man of words, preferring to let his actions speak for themselves instead. Which meant that he also didn't share much about himself with his children. Go figure.

Sure, she knew that her father liked her mother's *mee kuah* (everyone did), but she hadn't expected it to be his *favourite*.

"After your grandmother passed away before you were born, *Kakak* started making *mee kuah* for Raya every year," her aunt continues. "Partly for your father, and partly because she just thought it'd be a fun tradition to have."

"I see." Alya lets herself linger over the ruined recipe for a little longer. "Can I … can I have this recipe? Please?"

"Of course, you can!" Her aunt sounds astonished, like she doesn't understand why she's even asking. "But, I don't think I have your mother's recipe memorised. I guess I never saw a need to make it since she made it every year," she admits with a frown.

---

16 Love in Malay, also used as a term of endearment.

"Oh." Well, that was unfortunate. Alya ponders this as her eyes flit back to the recipe notebook. Despite what her aunt had just said, the beginnings of a plan were already starting to form in her head.

* * *

She tells Hakim about it before she returns to KL.

"You want to remake *Ibu*'s[17] *mee kuah* for *Abah*?" He asks. The fork full of scrambled eggs in his hand stops halfway to his mouth.

"Yep."

"With only half a recipe?"

"I'll manage, somehow."

"Alya." Her brother scrutinises her with an unimpressed look. "You can't cook."

"Rude."

"Have you ever touched a knife? Or made anything more elaborate than a bowl of instant noodles? How do you expect to recreate *Ibu*'s recipe?"

"Oh, ye of little faith," Alya sniffs. When her brother continues to level the same stare at her, she feels flustered. "I'll ask Dina for help!"

"Please do," he huffs, seconds before a genuine grin emerges. "But I'll admit, it's a nice idea. It'll be great if we can cheer up *Abah* somehow. Plus, I get to eat *Ibu*'s *mee kuah* during Raya again when I come back to KL. It's a win-win for all."

* * *

So, remaking her mother's recipe isn't as easy as Alya had expected.

She's sitting at the kitchen counter with her phone in front of her, looking at a snapshot of the ruined recipe in her aunt's recipe notebook. She doesn't have a clue where to start.

---

17 *Ibu* is mother in Malay.

"I guess the obvious answer would be the soup," she muses to herself. But what is the base? Shrimp stock? Beef stock?

"You good?" Dina materialises beside her to peer down at her phone's screen. She's already aware of Alya's plan, and is mildly sceptical about it even working out. But Alya's always been her family's token optimist. At the very least, Dina has agreed to help her out, only because she was worried about Alya burning down the kitchen if left unsupervised.

Dina pulls out her own phone. "Let's try comparing with other recipes first. There's only so many ways you can make *mee kuah*."

Many a night is then spent poring over *mee kuah* recipes online and comparing them with the original recipe. Sometimes, Alya would call up her aunt just to pick her brain about the possible ingredients to add into the soup, or if there was any specific way of cooking it.

"Stop trying to make it complicated!" Her aunt would berate Alya when she started going off on a tangent. "Good cooking isn't about fancy techniques, it needs plenty of love and care and time. Your mother knew this, too."

After the research comes the testing of the recipe. Sometimes they get carried away and cook late into the night, as that is the only time they are able to taste the soup due to the day-time fasting. After those nights, waking up for *sahur*[18] becomes even more of a struggle than it already is. Alya catches herself nodding into her pre-dawn meal more than once, while Dina stifles numerous yawns as they eat.

Hakim helps them foot the bill for all their experimentation (bones for stock and the other ingredients needed don't just grow on trees, after all). Sometimes while they cook, they'll call him up so he can look on, their brother tossing in unhelpful comments on occasion, *ooh-ing* and *aah-ing* whenever the results of their cooking

18 The early morning meal consumed by Muslims before fasting commences for the day.

look promising. Sometimes even after they are done cooking, they'd remain in the kitchen to chat, Dina updating her older siblings about university while Hakim dishes out gossip about his workplace. On those nights, the lonely air that had settled around their home is lifted, coloured by shared laughter and warmth.

All too soon, the final day of Ramadan arrives, bringing with it the familiar confusing mix of emotions that would rest in the hearts of all Muslims. While the passing of Ramadan is never not a sorrowful affair, there's also undoubtedly the excitement that comes with the promise of the following day.

Raya morning finds Alya and Dina clattering in the kitchen, hard at work as they prepare the noodles and toppings that would go with the soup. The batch of soup that's bubbling away on the stove has been deemed their best effort, the closest to what they hope is their mother's signature flavour.

Hakim appears in the kitchen moments later, just as Alya is slicing beef and shrimp. He'd returned to KL two days ago to help them out and stick around for the Raya festivities.

"Look at you, actually touching a knife," he teases.

"Quiet, you. Be useful and go set the table," she sniffs, turning back to the cutting board. Dina had left to fulfil the task of *somehow* getting their father downstairs to the dining table. Whether she'd be successful or not is a question that is very much up in the air.

"So demanding," Hakim gripes. Yet, he moves over to the tableware cupboard, procuring the necessary placemats and cutlery.

As Alya slices the ingredients, a torrent of thoughts swirl in her head. *What if* Abah *doesn't come down from his room? What if he doesn't like the* mee kuah? *What if this is all for nothing?*

What if he never comes back to us?

There are times when Alya walks past her father's bedroom and glances in, seeing the man who had raised her stare at the

TV listlessly from the armchair that has practically moulded itself to him.

And every single time, her heart turns into deadweight, in her chest.

Seeing her father turn into a shell of his former self was painful. It was as if when her mother had left them, she'd taken the part of him that could keep functioning with her.

She's jarred out of her thoughts when Hakim rushes back into the kitchen. "He's coming!" He hisses with wide eyes, as if he can't believe it himself. Alya rushes to bring the soup to the dining room as her brother grabs the rest of the toppings, setting everything on the dining table.

Footsteps sound on the staircase, and soon enough, their father appears downstairs, flanked by an anxious-looking Dina. He looks tired, the way he always does these days, dressed in a ratty T-shirt and a worn out *kain pelikat*.[19]

He takes in the sight of the dining table and his children waiting for him.

"Selamat Hari Raya, *Abah*," Alya says finally, smiling gingerly. "Raya wouldn't be Raya without *mee kuah*, and we heard that it was your favourite so … we made some. Just for you."

Her father looks at her for a long minute. His forehead wrinkles.

"Come on *Abah*, try some," Dina coaxes, as she gently guides him to take his usual seat at the head of the table. Once he does, the rest of them take their respective seats. Alya fixes her father a bowl of *mee kuah* before setting it in front of him.

Her father picks up his cutlery wordlessly; dipping his spoon into his bowl. All this while, Alya's acutely awware of the sound of her heartbeat thundering in her ears. Finally, her father sets his spoon down.

---

19 A chequered cloth that is worn around the waist by Malay men.

And pushes it away from him.

Alya's heart crashes into the pit of her stomach.

She watches as her father brings a hand up to cover his face. He sighs. It's long and heavy, and seems to hang in the air.

When he pulls his hand away to expose his face, his eyes are tearful.

She hears Hakim's sharp inhalation beside her. Across the table, Dina looks frozen, like she doesn't know what to do. Alya feels just as lost as she is.

Tears. She doesn't think she's ever seen her father cry. Not even when her mother died. Or at least, not in front of her. Yet here he is, his eyes filling as he exhales another sigh, this one shakier than the first. He clears his throat.

"It ..." His voice comes out rough, gravelly from lack of use. "It tastes just like your mother's."

Relief floods Alya's chest, so much so that she feels like she would burst. Dina beats her to it, bursting into tears as their father jerks towards her in alarm. Alya feels her own happy sob bubble up in her throat at the sight of her sister. She struggles to push it back down. Beside her, Hakim breaks into a relieved smile.

Their father is back. Whether for good or not, it doesn't matter. The important thing is that he is here with them now.

"Selamat Hari Raya, *Abah*," Dina burbles as she reaches over to clutch their father's hands, bringing them to her lips in a *salam*.[20] Alya and Hakim rise from their seats to come to their father's side.

"Selamat Hari Raya, *Abah*," they say, joining Dina as they take turns to *salam* their father's hand. "*Maaf zahir dan batin*."[21]

Their father smiles. It's a sad smile, small and watery. But it's tinged with fondness all the same.

---

20 A gesture of respect or affection, usually initiated by younger people towards their elders.
21 A common greeting during Eid in Malaysia, to ask others for forgiveness for any physical and emotional wrongdoings that one has committed.

"I'm the one who should be apologising for leaving you for an entire year," he says. "Selamat Hari Raya, my children, *maaf zahir dan batin*. Please forgive this negligent father of yours."

This time, Alya doesn't bother fighting back her tears. "We're just glad you're back, *Abah*," she sniffles, dashing her sleeve across her eyes. Hakim laughs at the sight, only to wince when he gets swatted by her.

There is so much left to address. So much left under the proverbial rug that they have to settle. As magic as their mother's *mee kuah* is, it isn't magic enough to resolve all their underlying issues with just a single taste.

But maybe for now, they can content themselves with this moment; with the sight of their father's slight smile as he watches his children over his bowl of *mee kuah*, Hakim laughing at his sisters as he passes them tissues so they can dry their tears and blow their noses.

There is so much left to be said, so much left to discuss. But that can wait. After all, Hari Raya is only just beginning.

Author's Note

As a child, and even now, Hari Raya Aidilfitri has always been a time I associate with some of my happiest moments. The dressing up, the food and the people. I wanted to convey the joy of coming together and surrounding yourself with the people you love and, of course, to honour my own mother's *mee kuah*, which is something I look forward to every single year.

While working on this story, I consulted family and friends for insight and proofreading, to see if my writing was able to convey the emotions that I wanted it to. Dialogue is particularly important, as it allows readers to notice nuances in the relationships of the characters: the doting way that Alya speaks to her sister, her brother Hakim's joking demeanour. Rather than describing how the characters feel, I describe their gestures and actions instead. Alya clutching the cushion out of anxiety is one example. The use of short sentences during scenes of heightened emotions helps to create tension and a sense of urgency.

Above all, I wanted to convey the message of not only family, but of love and the different ways that it is conveyed. Among the ways I have tried to convey this is through the use of imagery and flashback. I have also tried to show this through several instances in the story: the snapshot of Alya's parents at their wedding, the tireless way that she and her sister try to piece together the recipe, and even the grief that hangs over their father after their mother's passing. It's the idea that love is capable of breaking hearts, yet it is also able to mend them and make the family whole once more. For it is love that cripples Alya's family, but it is also love that brings them back together again.

The Many Painted Faces of Chinese Opera

Clara Mok

In Singapore, Chinese opera is known as "street show". It is an important part of Chinese cultural heritage. There are three main Chinese dialect groups in Singapore, the Hokkien, Teochew and Cantonese, with each of these groups having its own brand of Chinese opera.

Before radio and television came about, Chinese families had no other entertainment except Chinese opera. They would lug stools from their homes, walk to the nearest temple and sit facing the wooden stage as a live performance unfolded before their eyes.

This traditional Chinese dramatic form was brought to Singapore by China immigrants in the 19th century. It is staged outdoors on temple grounds as a form of respect during deities' birthdays and customary festivals. Such performances are free for the public as opera troupes are engaged by businessmen, temples and associations.

Chinese opera is performed on a makeshift wooden stage. A canopy supported by poles shelters the stage from the elements. The backstage area is separated from the main stage by a scenic backdrop. Each performer's makeup reflects the character traits being portrayed. A performer's costume consists of a headdress, robes, footwear and sometimes an artificial beard, which hints to the character's personality, gender and social status. Seated on both sides of the stage, musicians accompany the performers' singing and provide mood-setting background music.

With the Government's push to replace Chinese dialects with Mandarin, westernisation of the population, and an ageing and dwindling audience, Chinese opera lost its appeal among the Chinese community. In 2020, Singaporean youth got a glimpse into the lives of opera troupe members in a popular television serial, "Titoudao".

She dabs talcum powder on her face.

"Ling, take care of the troupe …" Madam Ang's icy cold hand cupped over Ling's dainty fingers. "Ah Peng can help but you're the one I trust most." Madam Ang's face turned ghastly white as she took her last breath. "Ah Ma!" cried Ling.

Madam Ang passed on a year ago, leaving Gek Lee Hokkien Performing Troupe in Ling's charge.

Ah Peng disappeared for days after that. Ling combed the alleys around their makeshift stage at Geylang. Finally, she found her brother-in-law slumped against a lamppost in a back alley overgrown with weeds, a can of beer in one hand, several crushed cans littered around him.

"Where have you been? We've things to discuss."

"Discuss? What's there to discuss? Mother is gone. You are her favourite … *hic* … you decide," Ah Peng said.

"Come on, be sober! I'm sure Mother won't want to see you like this," Ling chided.

Ah Peng waved off Ling and used the lamppost to prop himself up. As he tottered from the surge of alcohol in his blood, he tripped on a stone. "Ouch!" he cried, landing himself in a muddy mess.

Ah Ma in Heaven! Ling prayed. *Bless Ah Peng so that he comes to his senses.*

She layers on another coat of powder, her thoughts adrift.

Ling dabbed powder over the fine wrinkles which had started to form under her eyes, "Forty years on stage … time is not forgiving."

Her eyes moved to the photograph of Jerica, when she was six years old. She recalled how she had once sat on her lap at the steps of the stage and asked, "Mama, when did you start performing?"

"At 16. I was hooked by the magic of assuming another character on stage," she replied. "When you're older, I will let you play some roles on stage, OK?"

"I want to be a maid-in-waiting."

"A maid-in-waiting? Not a princess? A princess gets to wear beautiful gowns and headgear."

"You look so pretty as the princess, Ma. I want to be your maid-in-waiting. How come Pa doesn't act? He can be a king or general."

"Pa prefers working in the office."

When Jerica was 15, she got assigned to play little roles in the troupe. Once, her classmate spotted her backstage with her face covered in thick makeup. The classmate spread rumours that Jerica looked like a clown and soon the whole school knew about it. Jerica ran off the stage and cried for days.

What can I do? No matter how hard I try, she just refuses to come back to the troupe.

She applies a third layer of white powder.

Smoke swirled before Ling's stoic face as she clasped three incense sticks at the altar: "Gods, bless me with good health so I'm able to run the troupe for many years to come, or else the troupe may have to disband."

Gek Lee Hokkien Performing Troupe depended on private projects at various temples to finance itself, unlike amateur troupes which were backed by government funding.

If only we had government support, we would not need to worry so much. I'll put in our application again.

With her right hand, albeit unsteadily, she draws on the eyeliner with a purposeful slant on the outer eyelid.

"Wah! How come you lost weight or what, ah? Your costume is so loose!"

Ling overheard the light-hearted banter of Mei and other troupe members. Guilt knifed her in her heart. At 56, she had spent more than half of her lifetime in the troupe with Mei, who had joined the troupe at the same time.

I hope they understand I don't want to leave them …

She draws on her lip using a lip pencil, hands shaking slightly.

"How can she do that to me? She's my only child!" Ling moaned, beating her fist against her chest.

Mei listened intently as Ling narrated how Jerica brought her British boyfriend home. Before that, Ling did not even know that she was going steady with a foreigner. He did not know about Chinese customs. On the day he visited, he wore a black suit with black pants, a colour the Chinese believed to bring bad luck.

"He asked me for Jerica's hand in marriage."

"You understood what he said?" asked Mei.

"No, but he knelt down before me, pleading with me."

"Did you agree?"

"I chose to ignore him until …"

"Until?"

"Until Jerica knelt down too and asked me to let her pursue her happiness."

"Oh dear! Will they stay in Singapore or …"

"They will live in England!" Ling burst into tears, inconsolable.

If only Jerica would change her mind and marry a local! Ling prayed. May our ancestors forgive her!

She takes a deep breath, steadying her hand.

"Ma, come to England with me. I need someone to look after my baby," pleaded Jerica, who was five months pregnant.

"My troupe also needs me. Why don't you ask your mother-in-law?" said Ling.

"I can't stand her! How can I even ask her to look after my child? Please, Ma, I really need you," said Jerica.

Ling was like a servant with two masters. As a mother, she yearned to help Jerica tide over this difficult phase. Yet, she found it hard to be away from her troupe members, whom she had long regarded as family.

She fills in her lip colour, her brows knitted tightly.

"So hot! *Buay tahan*!"[1] Ling said. Her troupe members nodded warily.

Sweat trickled down her forehead as she busied herself sorting costumes in huge plastic boxes. Like rabbits from a magician's hat, the boxes stored glorious headdresses with pompoms, embroidered robes with trimmings, sequined sharp-toed shoes and artificial beards of grey, white and black.

The canvas sheets covering the top of the stage acted like a mega greenhouse roof trapping heat, making the makeshift wooden backstage area unbearably hot at midday. Powerful portable fans made the heat easier to bear as the performers put on makeup in preparation for the 2pm prayer ceremony at Tian Siak Keng Temple.

The clanking of cymbals brought a rousing start to the prayer ceremony to honour the deities. Decked out in full costumes and headgears, the entire cast of characters made a grand entrance onto the stage. Ah Peng led the cast in, circling the stage adorned with colourful flags and banners. The stage props consisted of two chairs and tables with a wine jar and several cups. Cymbals were crashed in perfect timing by the musicians.

In his bright red official's costume and holding his oversized belt, Ah Peng cut a dominant presence on stage. His strong

---

1 "Buay" means "cannot" in Hokkien while "tahan" means "withstand" in Malay, together the expression refers to an unbearable or intolerable situation.

masculine voice boomed in crisp Hokkien, "There isn't a time when flowers don't bloom …"

Under the direction of the temple staff, Ah Peng, Ling and Mei stood before each deity in the temple and kowtowed three times while offering incense, as the cymbals continued to clank in the background.

After this ritual, the show started. Whether there was an audience or not, the performance had to go on. After all, it was meant for the eyes of the deities.

On the last day of the performance, Ling withdrew a stack of $50 and $10 notes from the bank and distributed them to the troupe members.

"Here's for you, Mei."

Mei folded up the crisp notes with her thin fingers and placed them in her makeup case.

"Let's go and eat *dim sum*,"[2] someone suggested.

"*Dim sum*? No thanks!" Mei replied, opening her thermos flask and the fragrance of fresh porridge with salted egg wafted from it.

* * *

After the performance, Ling gathered all her troupe members backstage. They seemed an odd bunch as some of them still had makeup on but were dressed in modern clothes, while others had no makeup on but were still dressed in costumes of ancient clothes.

"I have an announcement to make. This is not easy, but as a mother, I have to do this. Jerica needs someone to help her cook and look after her baby in England. You know how reliant she is on me. I've a mother's duty to fulfil. I've to be away for six months, just six months, that's all I ask … and I'll be back."

---

2 Small bite-sized dishes that are served in bamboo steamer baskets or small plates in Chinese restaurants for breakfast or lunch.

"Who's going to arrange the schedules, the costumes, the performances?" someone voiced out.

"Don't worry. Mei and Peng will take over while I'm gone."

"Please don't leave us!" Mei cried.

"Yes, don't!" chimed in the troupe members.

"I can't bear to." Ling's voice broke, tears leaving a deep trail in her makeup.

Mei and the troupe members hugged Ling, sharing the sorrow of her impending departure.

She gives a deep sigh.

Squashing a can of beer in his hands, Ah Peng narrowed his eyes as he spat out, "Don't think you can get away with this, Ling. Mother in heaven must be cursing you now. What about the troupe? You place your own family first. What if we go bust? Some of us don't even have a day job. So, go!"

"Hey, watch your words, Peng. If I'm really like that, I wouldn't be so miserable now."

"You like to pretend. Think we don't know?"

"What's there to pretend? I'd told my daughter I won't go, but she insisted."

"See? You admit. She gives you money and you have a change of heart."

"A change of heart? What makes you think so? I put in as much effort into this troupe as everyone here, even more. By the time I lock up the costumes, it's already two in the morning. Have I ever let any of you down?" Ling said, her voice quivering.

"Really? We shall see," Ah Peng challenged. "Let's put this to a vote. Those who don't trust her, come stand by my side. Those who do, go stand by her!"

Forced to choose between Ah Peng's camp and Ling's camp, the troupe members were thrown into a quagmire.

Mei boldly stepped towards Ling.

"Hey, why do you support her, not me?" sneered Ah Peng. "She pays you more, ah?"

"Don't talk rubbish, Ah Peng. You know it's not true. I'm simply standing up for who I trust," Mei retorted.

A handful also sidled up to Ling's side, avoiding Ah Peng's gaze. Only two members took Ah Peng's side.

Ah Peng's face took on a murderous glint. "Ling, since so many of them support you, you must prove yourself."

"How?"

"Kneel down before the altar and swear to the Gods!"

"As if I don't dare to," Ling said as she glared at Ah Peng.

Standing before the ancestral altar, Ling lit three joss sticks and swore, "Dear Gods, I hereby swear that I'll be back and lead the troupe after six months. Should I break my promise, may I be struck by ..."

Mei wrenched the joss sticks from Ling and knelt down.

"Gods, I am willing to accept any punishment should Ling go back on her promise."

"Hey!" Ling stretched her arms to take back the joss sticks.

"Both of you gang up, is it? Right in front of the Gods! I won't let the matter rest so easily," snarled Ah Peng. "You wait and see."

Just then, a thick tree branch broke and collapsed on top of the canvas, causing part of the stage to collapse.

"What's happening?"

"Don't quarrel anymore. See, our ancestors are angry with us!"

She sticks on the false eyelashes.

The next day, the troupe members urged Ah Peng to apologise to Ling.

"Come on!" they cried.

He hovered around Ling as she did her makeup, her lips curled upwards. Ling pretended to ignore him.

"Er ... Ling ..." Ah Peng stammered.

"What?" snapped Ling.

"Well, I was too harsh, you know," Ah Peng said.

"Glad you know!" replied Ling. "Made me so angry until I couldn't sleep well. You have the cheek to ask the members to choose sides."

"You see ... I want to honour Mother's wish and keep the troupe going," Ah Peng explained. "It's OK to leave for a while. I'm sure everyone will help. What to do? Our role as parents comes first. We owe our children a debt in our previous lives."

Ling scowled and wanted to give Ah Peng a piece of her mind. Then she thought better of it and shook her head.

Ah Peng scratched his ear, "No hard feelings?"

"No hard feelings. We're family. No overnight feuds."

* * *

Ling's heart was tied in a knot. She was scheduled to fly the next day. Fondling costumes that she would not be wearing for months, tears welled up in her eyes.

"Come on, Ling. Don't be sad. You'll come back. I know you will," Mei said, as she hugged Ling. On Mei's bony shoulder, Ling's thick makeup was smudged by tears.

Before her departure, Ling busied herself handing over her numerous tasks to the troupe.

"No need to worry," reassured Mei. "You may not be with us physically, but you are in our hearts and we are in yours."

With that assurance, Ling's sobs gradually subsided.

"I'll be back for sure," said Ling.

She clips on her false hair with bobby pins.
Two weeks short of six months, Ling was drying the baby's nappies when she received a long-distance call from Mei.

"How are you, Ling?"

"Super *jiat lat!*[3] Like a slave, I'm doing housework, cooking three meals and looking after the baby, Matthew!" complained Ling. "Mei, I really miss all of you."

"Ling, you know I hate to disturb you but … we're in trouble here. Big-time trouble!"

"What happened?" Ling asked.

"Ah Peng must have been drinking when he got into a quarrel with Ouyang of Tian Siak Keng Temple! Ouyang cancelled our performances for September to November. What shall we do?"

"Trust Ah Peng to mess things up when I'm gone. Now the future of the troupe hangs in the balance. So foolish of him!" sighed Ling.

Ling paced about in Matthew's nursery as she contemplated her next move. Tian Siak Keng Temple was a major customer who engaged them for three major performances a year and was generous with the honorarium. Losing this customer meant a threat to the troupe's survival. The news had ignited an urgent need to fly back to Singapore.

* * *

Jerica came into the nursery.

"Let's talk outside. Don't disturb Matthew. I've an urgent matter to discuss with you," Ling said.

"Ma, you look worried."

"Ah Peng messed up and Tian Siak Keng's a big customer. Imagine losing 12 weeks of performances a year. How is our troupe going to survive? I must fly back immediately."

---

3   A difficult or dire situation.

"Ma, but Matthew has jaundice and the doctor says he must go under the sun every two hours. If you're not here, how am I going to cope?"

"Jerica, I promised Ah Mah on her deathbed to keep the troupe going. I cannot let her down. Why not fly over with me to Singapore for two months? We can look after Matthew together."

"Matthew is still so young. I'm not sure if he can stand the long flight to Singapore."

"I've no choice but to go back to talk to a close friend of Ouyang's. See if he can help."

"Ma, can't someone else in the troupe do that?"

"Sincerity is very important in our line of business. I have to pay him a personal visit."

"Ma, stay at least two more weeks while I look for a babysitter?"

"Afraid I can't, Jerica. The troupe may fold up if we don't win back the business. I cannot leave them like that."

"Stay for the sake of Matthew?"

"How about your neighbour next door? Can she be your babysitter?"

"I don't quite trust her."

"I really wish to help you but the six months is almost up already …"

"Okay, Ma. I know how important your troupe is to you. I will find a way to cope somehow."

"Trust your maternal instincts and you'll be fine."

With tears in her eyes, she bid Jerica and baby Matthew goodbye.

She puts on the crimson blusher with a broad brush.

Faces expectant, the troupe members eyed Ling as she stepped up the ladder attached to the wooden frame of the stage. Earlier, she had met up with Ouyang.

"How is it, Ling?" asked Ah Peng. "Come on. Tell us!"

Ling's face was taut. "What do you think happened?"

Ah Peng pleaded, "It's my fault. I shouldn't have been so rash. Tell us, please."

"I talked to Ouyang's friend who managed to persuade Ouyang to give the slots back to us. Our prayers to the ancestors have been answered."

Ah Peng's knitted brows relaxed. His eyes, heavy from lack of sleep, brightened. Laughter rippled through the troupe once again. The troupe members bowed before the altar. "Thank you, Gods!"

* * *

"Ling, I can't believe it. Government is giving us $3,000 a year!" Mei said.

"Really?" Ling asked.

"It says here in the letter: '*Gek Lee Hokkien Performing Troupe* is invited to perform at the refurbished Victoria Theatre. With the grant and new performing venue, *Gek Lee Hokkien Performing Troupe* is expected to reach out to the mass audience and educate the young generation about Chinese opera and culture.'"

"Show it to me," asked Ling. Her furrowed brows relaxed as she read the letter, "We've applied for this funding so many times. Finally!" Ling exclaimed, letting out an audible sigh.

When she shared the news with her troupe mates, they rejoiced. "Yeah! We've a chance to perform on a proper stage at last!"

She checks herself in the mirror. The look is complete.

The transformation of Ling's hair was spectacular. With a few strokes, a mop of long hair was attached to her current shoulder-length hair, held in place by bobby pins. Donning a tall headdress with pompoms and a snow-white gown with sequins, Ling dazzled on stage as the well-known White Snake Maiden with a tragic tale to tell.

Adorned with colourful flags, banners and wispy mist, the stage came alive with lines sung in perfect pitch and cymbals sounded in perfect timing. The performers' voices were crystal clear, accentuated by the tip-top acoustics at Victoria Theatre.

Ling's strong yet feminine vocals lilted as her character endured a cruel fate of separation from her beloved. She was imprisoned in a pagoda by the evil abbot who wielded his staff against White Snake Maiden's sworn sister, the Green Snake. An action-packed fight sequence ensued with the Green Snake emerging victorious, thus freeing White Snake Maiden to reunite with her mortal husband.

Wowed, the audience gave the troupe a standing ovation for their performance of "The Legend of Madam White Snake".

Sharing the joy with Ling backstage were Jerica and baby Matthew.

Author's Note

My interest in Chinese opera was piqued when my maternal grandparents brought me to watch Teochew opera. The glittering costumes and props – swords and spears – fascinated me. With the advent of television, Chinese opera faded into the background.

It was on a rainy morning in 2016 that I greeted the troupe members of Seow Hong Hokkien Wayang. They had invited me for their performance near a flatted factory. Despite its remote location, I went down to interview the troupe mistress, Qiaoyun. She shared about her life and how she ran her troupe. Her tenacity and leadership inspired me.

I was determined to craft a story with her as the main protagonist. She had married the son of the troupe's previous "mistress" (just like Ling in my story) and had children. I was touched by the warm camaraderie between her troupe members. Then I began to postulate different scenarios which would tear her away from them.

The essential writing skill for this story is observation. I had to immerse myself in the sights and sounds of the performing troupe. Climbing up the rickety ladder to observe the performers backstage in their glittering costumes and headgear is a far cry from passively watching them perform on stage.

I observed the troupe members backstage whenever I had the chance to do so. I watched the actresses in various stages of makeup application and costume changes before they stepped onto the stage. Once, I caught Qiaoyun distributing a stack of notes to her troupe members and was inspired to write about it. During an afternoon prayer session, I saw first-hand how the performers offered incense to the gods in their elaborate costumes. My T-shirt was soaked through as I followed them. I cannot imagine how stuffy it must be in those double-layered, long-sleeved costumes. These details added a touch of realism to my story.

Backstage, I noticed how meticulous it was for troupe members to do their makeup. Since this is an essential part of Chinese opera, I incorporated the steps of their makeup to tie up the entire story.

"The Many Painted Faces of Chinese Opera" is a labour of love for an art form which is fast diminishing in Singapore and my role as a writer is to bring it to the forefront for all to appreciate.

I am thankful to Seow Hong Hokkien Wayang's troupe members who granted me unlimited VIP backstage access to view and admire their priceless collection of costumes, headgears and accessories.

Itterasshai – Go Well and Come Back

Maureen SY Tai

The Japanese say "*Ittekimasu!*" (I'll go and come back) when they leave their homes for work, school or a trip, and those left behind will respond with "*Itterasshai!*" (Go well and come back). When the Japanese come home after being away, they'll call out "*Tadaima!*" (I'm safely here now) and whoever's home will reply "*Okaerinasai!*" or "*Okaeri!*" (Welcome back).

These four simple words, spoken ritualistically with each departure and return, mean more than just a simple "hello" and "goodbye". Within is a deeper meaning, a warmth and a hope, that the departing person will return to the point of departure, safe and well, and that those left at home will be waiting for that person to return. These words imply that the place you have just left is a place where you belong, where you are loved, that you call home, that you would never abandon, and that you wish to return to its comforting fold. These words and this practice, in their nuanced simplicity, exemplify some of the more distinctive Japanese traits: attention to detail, depth of thought and economy of words.

As I have become older, possibly wiser, I realise that each utterance of "*Ittekimasu*" or "*Itterasshai*" is additionally tinged with melancholy. After all, once one has left, there is no guarantee that one will be able to return home. But there is always hope, even in the darkest of circumstances. With every "*Ittekimasu!*", we hold on to that hope, waiting for that life-affirming moment when we cross the threshold on return and cry "*Tadaima!*" as joyously as we can.

Winter

I'm wearing my mother's coat. It smells faintly of mothballs, despite having been hung in the blazing Malaysian sun for days. A row of older Japanese men mill about awkwardly at a distance from me, talking amongst themselves in a language that I don't yet understand. The syllables are short and choppy, and the nod of the head seems to double as punctuation. The only woman in the welcoming party is also the only person who speaks some English. She introduces herself as my host mother, the matriarch of the first of four families that I'll live with this year. She fusses around me like a hen with her chick, making sure I have all my bags (one large suitcase, my father's), my papers (Malaysian passport, in hand) and that I'm not hungry (I am, and I remember my *kaya*[1] butter sandwich in my backpack).

We are standing at the arrival hall in Narita Airport. It is December 1988. I've just arrived in Tōkyo as a Rotary Club exchange student, committed to spending an entire year in Japan as a sort of cultural attaché. I don't know it yet, but in less than two weeks' time, Emperor Hirohito will be dead and the Heisei Era will begin. Right now, my eyes are bloodshot and puffy from crying almost the entire flight over. I've never been away from my family before and I've never felt more homesick.

Stranger

I sit cross-legged on my narrow bed in my narrow cell of a bedroom. My suitcase is too big for the under-bed storage space, so it covers the entirety of my desk. It is only half unpacked, a stark reminder that I'm just a transient visitor, an "alien" or *gaijin*[2] as I'm called in Japanese. I stare at the *Nihongo*[3] *for Beginners* textbook on my lap. It teaches me to tell the time and how to ask where the toilet is, but doesn't give me the words to say "It's not that I don't like the food, but I can't eat because my stomach is a knotted ball of sadness" or "I feel like a prisoner in your home even though I know this is an ungrateful way to be" or "I can't even tell the shampoo

---

1 A sweet spread for bread or toast made with coconut milk and eggs.

2 Foreigner.

3 Japanese (language).

from the conditioner, or the laundry detergent from the floor cleaner"! I look helplessly at the words. Their meaning is hidden, undecipherable from the jumble of lines and ticks. I start to cry. I hear my host mother's slippered feet stop outside my door, and after a pause, they pad away softly, almost apologetically.

Homesick

My biological father sighs. Not a good sign. He tells me that their last telephone bill cost as much as a return plane ticket from Malaysia to Japan for two. My stomach sinks as I reluctantly agree to limit my collect calls to emergencies. After I hang up, I ask my host mother where the closest post office is.

Depressed

My first experience of winter is dark and miserable, not at all romantic or cosy as I'd imagined. There are no fireplaces in front of cosy armchairs in this sprawling metropolis. Just convenience stores and vending machines, buildings of glass and steel, and trains that rumble interminably across the skyline. *It is impossible to live in a place that is so hard and cold.* I look at the sentence I've just written and crumple the paper into a ball.

Gakkō – School

In February, I start my daily commute to language school, where our group of foreign exchange students are expected to master the basics of the three types of Japanese script: *hiragana*, *katakana* and *kanji*.[4] I sit next to Karina from Australia, the tallest white girl I've ever met. She says she has big feet and a big nose. I agree. Karina quickly establishes herself as the best student in the class, with an infectious thirst for life. Hardly

---

4 The three sets of characters used in the Japanese written language.

two weeks into school, however, she's mean to me, calling me a "hopeless grommet" and demanding loudly why I'm in Japan if all I ever do is cry miserably into my *bentō*[5] at lunchtime. I can't find "grommet" in my pocket Oxford English Dictionary, but it sounds like a slimy grub, something you flick away in disgust when you find it crawling up your arm. I never find out why Karina bothered to talk to me at all. Everyone else avoids me and I don't blame them. Even my host family treads on eggshells around me as I mope about their tiny apartment like a wounded animal. Karina's words slap me in the face and I wake up. I speak English, Bahasa Malaysia and Cantonese fluently. I'm not letting this atonal language defeat me.

Sotsugyō – Graduation

For the past three weeks, I've channelled my inner geek towards the dedicated study of Japanese. Karina and I spur each other on as we compete for the honour of being crowned *Nihongo Master* of our class. We study together after school and curl our tongues around the new words at every opportunity. We refuse to be embarrassed by our mistakes, which are plentiful. It helps that the Japanese are the politest and most patient people in the world, smiling amiably at us even as we attempt to clumsily string sentences together at the bakery or at one of the hundreds of 7-Eleven shops near our language school.

Towards the end of the month-long course, I feel more like myself than I have in months, and Karina and I are jointly bestowed the coveted *Nihongo Master* title. On the last day, all the foreign exchange students gather for a final photograph (one of the thousands taken over the year). We stand in a line, smile and chant "*chī-zu*" in unison – which is how the Japanese say "cheese" – one final time. I tell my Amazonian Aussie that I hope we'll

---

5   Lunch box.

still be friends even after we disperse to different high schools in Tōkyo. She says we'll be best friends. I don't know it yet, but I'm right to believe her.

Kyōdai – Siblings

My host family takes me to Disneyland. I'll be moving to my second host family's house in the middle of March, and this is their way of saying farewell. In between rides, Kaoru shows me how to play cat's cradle with a length of yarn while Mihoko draws *manga*[6] girls with impossibly large eyes in her notebook. I look up the word "impossible" in my English-Japanese dictionary (Sanseido edition, my host mother's) and Mihoko looks at me quizzically as I say the word, jabbing at her pictures. I write it down in my notebook, *fukanō*.[7] It may come in useful yet. Mayumi is just two, the youngest of the three sisters, with ruddy cheeks that I want to pinch, but don't. She hides away from me in *okāsan*'s[8] skirt. I have to call my host mother *okāsan* too, one of the many Rotary Club rules that we exchange students are required to abide by. Because it is a foreign language, I don't feel guilty, but I'll only ever have one mother, even though she is too far away. I bury my face in the folds of my navy coat and breathe in the fading scents of home.

Hanami – Flower viewing

I help my second host mother spread the red and white chequered cloth on the grass as her children clamber up the gnarled trunk of the *sakura*[9] tree. There is still a chill in the air, but it is light and playful, mingling with the laughing voices of families and friends marvelling at the sight of blushing cherry blossoms overhead. My

---

6 Japanese comics.
7 Impossible.
8 Okāsan is mother in Japanese.
9 Cherry blossom.

host mother and I chatter as we lay out our lunch of *sushi*[10] and freshly baked buns. She can't speak any English, but she corrects my Japanese remorselessly and tirelessly, and I am grateful for that.

She is asking me about the Rotary Club rules, all the things that I'm not allowed to do during my year in Japan. "*O-sake nomu koto dekinai?*"[11] she asks, and I nod. Absolutely, the drinking of alcohol is strictly prohibited. "*Kuruma, dame,*"[12] I say, making a cross with my two index fingers. No driving either. "*Boifurendo mo, dame.*"[13] Romantic liaisons are most definitely a no-no. My host mother nods sympathetically. "*Soreya, taihen da ne,*"[14] she agrees. I don't tell her that I don't feel oppressed at all since I've never had any of these prohibited experiences before and am not planning to, not this year anyway. I look up and I'm blinded by the pink clouds. I close my eyes and enjoy the smile playing on my lips.

Yamete kudasai – Please stop

Karina tells me about these sleazy, unsavoury characters, *chikan*[15] as they are called in Japanese. Despicable men who take advantage of being in close proximity to women, even young girls, on trains and who wordlessly grope females who have been rendered immobile by the packed crowds. I listen, open-mouthed, to Karina's account of how she manages to free her pinioned arm and slap her assailant in his face after he brazenly grabs her. Her eyes blaze jubilantly. I'm filled with pride at her bravery but also dread. What if some unknown man tries that on me? What would I do, how would I feel?

---

10 A traditional Japanese dish made of vinegared rice, seaweed and a variety of raw seafood.
11 You can't have alcohol?
12 No driving.
13 No boyfriends, either.
14 That's tough (a sympathetic comment).
15 Person who makes unwelcome advances, typically on a train.

I try not to think about it as I stand on the platform in the lingering spring cold. For the first time, I baulk at the packed carriage, the passengers squeezed so closely together that there is no space at all between individuals. I try to swallow my fear but my feet refuse to move. I'm not sure how long I stand there, feeling the rush of air from passing trains, listening to the cheerful voice announcing the opening and closing of doors, waiting for a safe space on the train home.

Kimochi warui – A bad feeling

My real mum asks me how I am, really. *Is there an emergency?* I twirl the telephone cord around my finger. *I just wanted to hear your voice, Mum, that's all.* I think I sound upbeat but she isn't fooled. My real dad calls a few hours later, asking if I want to come home. I shake my head and say no, even though every cell in my body is pleading the exact opposite.

Tomodachi – Friends

The end of *kagaku* or science. The girls in my class hurriedly take out oversized hair rollers from their black handbag-style school bags and curl their fringes. I give up trying to concentrate as they flit about, giggling and chattering in falsetto voices. The new Checkers album, "Seven Heaven", has just been released and everyone is learning the songs. I love it, too. Fumiya Fujii, the group's lead singer, has replaced my previous crush, Noriyuki Higashiyama of the boy band Shōnentai, who was, embarrassingly, the main reason why I applied to be a Rotary exchange student in the first place.

I put away my notebooks with their rows and rows of *kanji* and sit with Aya, Naoko, Yuko and Fumio. The girls are in the school *kendō*[16] club that I joined a few weeks ago. Unlike the others,

---

16 A Japanese form of fencing.

they have unquestioningly accepted me into their group. I don't know how lucky I am. They chat about last night's episode of the comedy *Tunnels* and next week's *Top Ten* show that features the current, most popular pop songs in Japan. I can just about make out every eighth word they say these days, constantly interjecting with my "*Nani? Imi wakaranai!*"[17] They stop just as often to explain and then patiently watch me write the new words down in my notebook. Most of the useful stuff that I learn from them are colloquialisms, used daily, and not found in my dictionary or textbooks. Printed sources have serious limitations when it comes to learning a living language. The best teachers are the people around me, and my best learning tools are my eyes, ears, tireless writing hand and ridiculously thick skin.

Omoide – Memories

My best friends from home send me a cassette tape, wrapped in seemingly unending layers of newspaper, like the secret gift in the game of "Passing the Parcel". The girls have gathered for a last hurrah before Jing leaves for Singapore as an ASEAN scholar, and they record themselves as a birthday present for me. They are in Jing's house, stuffing themselves with *murukku*[18] and prawn crackers, I just know it. Wei Li asks me a whole raft of questions before Winnie reminds her that I can't possibly answer. Peng Peng teases Mei Wai about her crush on a Hong Kong movie star, and Sujata is accused of harbouring dreams of running away with a goat herder. They dissolve into gales of laughter. Side B of the tape is 30 minutes of private messages from each of them – quiet, sombre monologues filled with longing for our carefree high school days and fear for what the future holds for each of us as we go our separate ways. It will be many years before I am able to listen to the tape again without bawling my eyes out.

---

17 What? I don't understand!
18 A deep fried, crunchy Indian snack.

Karada ga itai – My body is aching

I sign up for my high school's week-long *kendō* summer camp, largely because my friends persuade me to. They tell me excitedly that the boys from the separate Gakushuin boy's school will also be in attendance. We've never had joint practices before so I don't know what to expect. The first day is gruelling. We wake at 5am, and after tidying up our *futons*,[19] we head to breakfast and then to practice. I'm a newbie and unranked, so I'm lumped with the younger children while my friends are grouped with their peers. Whether the little ones stare at me in wonder or fear, it's hard to tell. I feel like Gulliver among the Lilliputians. As the stern-faced *sensei*[20] glide into the *dōjō* or practice hall, their stiff *hakama* or *kendō* pants making swishing sounds against the wooden floors, the eyes of even the youngest children take on a steely gaze. Their focus is unwavering.

We practice all day long, our bare feet sliding purposefully along the polished floors, our arms aching from the overhead swing of the *shinai* or bamboo staff, our throats sore from the guttural war cries that we are forced to emit. I almost fall asleep during my dinner of rice, grilled mackerel and *misō*[21] soup. By the second day, my feet are blistered and so many parts of my body bruised from poorly defended *shinai* attacks that I give up trying to locate all the blue-black patches. I sneak peeks at my friends as we soak our bodies in the communal *ofuro* or bath. I'm relieved that they are just as battered and bruised, if not more so. "*Tanoshii?*"[22] asks Fumio, as we stroll back to our rooms. I nod, but only because I am too beat to say anything else.

---

19 Japanese-style mattresses.
20 Teacher(s).
21 A fermented soybean paste.
22 Fun?

Hatsukoi – First love

It's the last day of camp when I see Nanri *kun*[23] take off his helmet, unwind the sweat-soaked *tenugui*[24] wrapped around his head, and run his slender fingers through his dark, spiky hair. Unexpectedly, butterflies flutter furiously around in my stomach and my heart starts thumping in my ears like the barrel-shaped *taiko* drums in a festival. By the end of the summer, I'll have mastered writing Nanri *kun*'s full name in the margins of my notebooks.

Semi no nakigoe – The song of cicadas

I'm measured for a *yukata* or summer kimono in my third host family's living room. I stand barefoot on the *tatami*[25] in my underclothes as the bespectacled man measures me. He takes a look over his glasses, muttering "*Dekai na!*" under his breath, which I know roughly translates to "Holy cow, she's huge!" A few days later, I wear my brilliantly coloured *yukata* to the summer festival at the local shrine a few streets away. Karina has come along for a sleepover, my first in Japan. My third host sister, who is a decade older, laughingly pulls us into the conga line and we follow her in a traditional dance with *uchiwa* or fans in our hands. We giggle as I totter in my *geta*, wooden clogs that had to be custom made for me. My feet are apparently also "*dekai na*"!

We tuck into skewers of grilled chicken and my favourite *takoyaki* – grilled octopus balls – nestling in a tray, sold at the brightly lit stalls that line the sides of the temple compound. "*Irrasshai, irrasshai, irrasshai!*"[26] the vendors call out to everyone and no one in particular, their voices wafting into the humid night air. We walk home later that evening to the serenade of cicadas, my right arm comfortably linked with my host sister's and my left

---

23 Honorific term used to address young males.

24 Japanese hand towel.

25 A type of woven straw mat used as flooring in Japanese houses.

26 A welcome salutation, typically called out by vendors to customers.

arm with Karina's. I'm humming contentedly when I suddenly realise I've not written home in weeks.

Komaru – Confusion

I don't realise how much I've missed school and my friends until after the summer holidays. My *kendō* crew are now in their final year of high school, and at the pinnacle of the school totem pole. Aya, the most headstrong of the four, decides that the *kendō* clubs from both the girls' and boys' schools should have joint practices at least twice a month and go out for an early supper together afterwards. Everyone agrees and, miraculously, the *sensei* approves of her suggestion. Today, we decide to forego dinner for airy sweet pastries at the Mister Donut chain of cafés. Nanri *kun* remembers that I like the soft cruller that's half chocolate and half cream, and gallantly secures the last one in the display case for me. As we file upstairs to the seating area, Naoko jabs me with her elbow, hissing "*Deshou? Suki desuyo!*"[27] For the rest of the day, I cling to the thought of that last lonely doughnut as evidence of Nanri *kun's* affection for me. Could it be true?

Otera bakkari – Many temples

The *momiji*, or autumn leaves, create a breath-taking backdrop. I'm on a school trip to Nara and I should be *ooh-ing* and *aaah-ing* (or at least gazing reverently) at Kōfukuji, one of the oldest and most famous temples in the whole of Japan. Instead, I am sharing a pair of earphones with Sarah, the other Rotary exchange student at Gakushuin. She's an Aussie, like my best friend Karina. We are listening to our favourite – actually, our only – Checkers tape on her Walkman, remembering the concert that we went to at the Budōkan earlier this summer. My *kendō* friends had pooled

---

27 See? He likes you!

their money together and bought us tickets. I'd never been to a concert before, ever. I didn't even know what to wear (no blazers or pantyhose necessary, thank goodness). It was amazing. Sarah and I screamed "*I love you, Fumiya!*" as he was singing a ballad, and a good-natured wave of laughter rippled through the arena. It was very un-Japanese behaviour, just as we are exhibiting now, heads so close that they touch.

We listen to "Friends and Dream", a song about growing up and parting. I try not to think too hard about the time of year. I've only three months left of my exchange.

Sutekina namae deshō? – Isn't it a beautiful name?

I listen to the regular breathing of the others sleeping in the *tatami* room. Miyoshi, my fourth host mother, takes long sighing breaths whereas her grandchildren, Yasu and Junko, have shorter, more energetic intakes and outtakes of air, even in deep slumber. I don't remember the last time I slept in the same room with my own mother, and I suddenly feel guilty, realising I can't remember the last time I wrote a letter home either. A few days ago, I reprimanded my host father (after bringing him his suppertime bottle of beer) and told him not to use "Oi!" anymore when calling for his wife. "She has a lovely name and you should use it," I admonish. He looks at me in surprise, and softens, his eyes twinkling mischievously. "Like this, 'Miyoshi dear'?" "Yes, like that." We laugh, and my host mother tears up.

Later, she asks if I'd like to sleep with her in her room as it's warmer than my room downstairs. "There is space for another futon," she says, her voice hopeful. When the kids hear that I'm moving upstairs, they clamour for a sleepover. It turns out there is space for *four* futons. Yasu suddenly kicks me in the back, and I grimace, but only momentarily. I fall asleep, dreaming in a new tongue. I'm floating in a pink haze, encircled by doughnuts with gossamer wings that hover around me like hummingbirds, trying desperately to kiss my cheeks.

Eki de no kuchizuke – A kiss at the station

Nanri *kun* sheepishly offers to walk me to the subway station after the *kendō* club dinner gathering. Aya and the girls literally shove me out of the *okonomiyaki*[28] restaurant, giggling and whispering "*Gambatte ne!*"[29] I'll need all the luck I can get. I've chatted with Nanri *kun* before and after practices, but never, ever on my own. My feet are wobbly and my Japanese is even wobblier as we weave our way through the crowds. Nanri *kun* has to repeat his invitation to have ice cream three times before I understand what he's saying. "I've an hour before my 9:30pm curfew, so we'll have to hurry," I say. We share an ice cream parfait and fall into easy conversation about our *kendō* coaches and the rest of the team, the latest television dramas, my host families and his obsession with fishing. We play-fight with our long ice cream spoons.

In front of the ticket gate at the station, Nanri *kun* and I stand opposite each other, keeping a respectable distance between us so that we can comfortably bow goodbye, as I know proper, well brought-up Japanese teenagers should do. However, I'm not a Japanese teenager but a *gaijin* living on borrowed time and with nothing to lose. Before my mind can get in the way, I hastily stand on tiptoe and brush my lips against his, before bolting through the ticket gate and up the stairs onto the platform. I don't stop until I'm right at the end of the platform, my entire body flushed and beating to the rhythm of my pounding heart. I spend the rest of the night smiling into my pillow and kissing the soft skin on the back of my hand. I've broken a Rotary Club rule, but in that moment of delirious bliss, I couldn't care less.

---

28 A savoury pancake.
29 Good luck!

Yurushimasu – I forgive you

There is an old photograph in my host father's room of when he was a soldier in the Japanese army. We don't talk much about history or politics, mostly because my vocabulary has not evolved to that sophisticated level of discourse. We're watching a variety show after a home-cooked meal of *tonkatsu*, or deep fried pork cutlet, when he suddenly sits up and gazes at me. His eyes are brimming. "I am sorry," he says, slowly and deliberately, as if he has been rehearsing this for months. "For the war, and for what we did," he continues. I'm silent, uncertain of what to say. I'm not sure it's right for me to accept his apology on behalf of the thousands of Malayans who had suffered at the hands of their Japanese occupiers. I look at my hands, folded in my lap, and then I look at the man – the Rotarian, the soy sauce maker, the father, the grandfather – who has taken me into his home and accepted me as part of his family. It is within my ability to forgive him, and I do. That night, he snores louder than I've ever heard.

Shinyū – Best friend

Karina and I are wearing matching sweaters that we found in a discount shop in Harajuku last week. On each of our bellies is a print of a large smiling onion against a light pink background. Christmas isn't a big deal in Tōkyo. If it wasn't for the cute Santa displays in the department store windows or the jingling of sleigh bells in the seasonal television commercials, you'd miss it entirely.

As we open our presents from each other, we commiserate. Karina misses her turkey dinner with her family in Coffs Harbour, and I miss midnight mass with mine at our church in Ipoh. I break a Meiji chocolate bar in two and Karina pops open two bottles of Calpis. We spend the afternoon watching a cheesy episode of some romantic drama on television. I don't say it to her now, but

I tell her at the airport two weeks later as we cling to each other, before she gets on the plane bound for home, that this year has been the most life-changing of all my years alive on this planet, and I'll miss her more than anyone I've ever missed before. I've an inkling that my waterworks department will be working overtime during the remainder of my days in Japan.

Sayōnara no itami – The pain of goodbye

It's January 1990. I'm the last exchange student from my year to leave, so only my Japanese families and friends are at the airport to see me off. I'm not sure if my heart can endure any more breakages. Nevertheless, I feel like a rock star. My host families are there in full strength: the Seo's, the Otsuka's, the Suzuki's and the Yoshida's; my *kendō* friends; my first boyfriend; my friends from Rotex, the group of returning Japanese exchange students who have become my brothers and sisters; my *sadō* (tea ceremony), *ikebana* (flower arranging), *nihonga* (painting), *yokobue* (flute) and *Nihongo* teachers. My Seo host dad jokes that I'm more Japanese than the typical Japanese teenager. My real dad thinks I now qualify to be a *geisha* but stresses in an earlier letter that he does not encourage this as a career option. I'm sobbing as I say *"Ittekimasu"* and I hear the choked responses of *"Itterasshai"*.

Déjà vu. I'm wearing my mother's coat. I don't know it yet, but I'll cry almost the entire flight home.

Author's Note

"Itterasshai" is a story I've always wanted to tell but have found difficult to commit to paper because it's largely a recollection about real people living real lives in a real place. This time, when I sat down to try again, I gave myself permission to stray a little from the truth and to take some artistic liberties. Once I was able to put some healthy distance between myself and my teenage self who had been a foreign exchange student in Japan, the floodgates opened. The writing flowed easily, and the process, which had been torturous before, became extremely enjoyable. The story that resulted was a mix of nostalgic memoir and creative fiction (I'll leave you to guess which part is which), written in the present tense because it felt right to be told that way, perhaps so that with each reading, I could relive that year again and again, like in the movie "Groundhog Day".

Verification was another challenge to writing about a time in the pre-Internet past. Human memory is malleable and inherently unreliable. Thankfully, the Japanese were technologically superior even in the late 1980s and obsessed with photo-taking, so I had boxes of photo albums, videos and cassette tapes with all the facts recorded, accurate and fresh. My diaries were also useful resources for memory-mining. In the yellowed pages, I discovered events and observations that seemed insignificant back then, but when revisited with new eyes, went on to inspire a poem, a drawing, even a story (but I'll be honest, most of the entries were toe-curlingly cringey).

Writers are always asked where they get their ideas from. My humble answer is this: there are ideas everywhere around us, shimmering like sea-tossed shells on a sandy beach. You just have to be willing to look, seek them out, collect them, treasure them and then create your own personal art from them.

After all these years, I still adore Tokyo, despite its underbelly (the groping incident that Karina describes in my story was, and continues to be, a grim reality for many young female commuters). It always amazes me how the metropolis has changed so much, but yet remains at its core old, wise, kind, aloof and uniquely Japanese. Every time I visit, I am 18 again. When I leave, I whisper "*Ittekimasu*" under my breath, and I mean it, with all of my being.

The Shadow of her Smile

Tripat Narayanan

Sikh families in Malaysia in the 1960s and 1970s placed utmost importance on education while maintaining a cultural status quo within their Sikh religious and cultural way of life.

Pitted within this socio-cultural Sikh upbringing, daughters of upwardly mobile educated professional Sikh families were often schooled in English in the best colonial convents run by Irish nuns. At home and in family circles they were Punjabi Sikh, going to *gurdwaras*[1] on Sundays, and making roti and Punjabi chai as their set chores. But often these girls would have read a whole range of English literary classics growing up, while also watching every Hindi movie and popular Hollywood movies with family or friends. Many among them were accustomed to the educated professional elders in their families being all suited and booted with bow ties, socialising at drinks and dinner parties with other professionals and English colonial bosses.

Most families had a traditional outlook and romantic liaisons outside of parental arrangements were essentially forbidden, and were not discussed or encouraged. Intra-family romantic and marital connections were also frowned upon in the Punjabi Sikh culture. This originates from strong brethren connections within villages in rural agricultural Punjab of old, where young boys and girls were raised as brothers and sisters in each village.

The late 1960s and 1970s were, however, a time of worldwide change. Repressed, undemocratic attitudes of those in control were being questioned, as the younger generations rebelled. In today's more global world, some of the traditional customary Sikh outlooks are less upheld.

Every school holiday, Chani and her brothers were sent to an aunt's house down south in Singapore or up north to an uncle's

---

1 Places of worship for Sikhs.

in Perak. There was no questioning a decision made. There was just no questioning anything. And so it happened that Chani and her brothers spent many December holidays at Hunter Uncle's house in Kampar.

Here they passed their days with a riot of cousins. They would play house, role-playing the inner lives of the homes they lived in. Everyone would jostle to be the father and nobody ever wanted to be the child. A world ruled by only girl cousins on the cool sands under the wooden floors of the house on sturdy stilts, where admittance by height ensured no one beyond the age of 12 would enter this private world. Sometimes they played "catching", where boy cousins were allowed, on fenceless slopes of green, and picking fallen frangipanis and clean stones to make up new games. They also played hopscotch for hours on end, jumping to and fro. And staying out for as long as possible until diminishing light, mosquitoes and calling mothers forced them indoors to bathe, eat and make bed on the wooden floor of the large living room upstairs. There, they lay cousin to cousin, head to toe, on bare sheets sharing pillows, teasing and telling tales until sleep captured all.

One December, when Chani was suddenly 17, she and her younger brother were sent to their uncle's house soon after her Higher School Certificate (HSC) exams. This time, the girls were told they would be in the first bedroom, separate from the boys in the hall. There they dressed up to go nowhere, put on makeup, teased their hair tall, put *dupattas*[2] on their heads and sang Hindi songs. They talked about boys who were non-existent, tall, handsome, fair, clever – boys not like their fathers or uncles. Rather boys like Hindi film heroes, who would charm them off their feet someday.

One weekend that trip, the girls were packed off to Ipoh to visit an ailing grandmother. Chani had never before been to

2 A long scarf-like cloth worn over the head by Indian women.

the home of her cousin's maternal grandparents. It turned out that grandma, Maa-ji, was less ailing and more endearing. There were also a couple of extended family cousins, who were second cousins to her own cousins. There was one in particular who was also young, maybe 18, who laughed, teased and joked like a friend. He was no Hindi film hero, though. He was thin, dark and not even tall, but he quoted poetry and said clever things. He told Chani that he would foretell her future if she showed him her palm. Chani held out her hand and ever so gently, Prem barely brushed her hand as he told her tall tales of a happy tomorrow. Maa-ji watched a blooming Chani and an enchanted Prem with a vague sense of foreboding. Chani chatted on quite unaware that her chiffon *dupatta* had slipped a little and her sleeveless *churidar kameez*[3] enticed the onlooker further.

Later when her cousins teased her in the bedroom, Chani was all aflush.

"Prem likes you," they said to her.

She caught a glimpse of herself in the mirror across the room – looming brown eyes in a fine-featured serene face.

"I am pretty," she thought, pushing tendrils of stray hair behind her ears.

Prem accompanied the girls back to Kampar. He was due to leave for Kuala Lumpur, on route to England for further studies. At Kampar, he was commissioned to escort Chani and her little brother back to Kuala Lumpur. Never had a train ride been so wondrous before. Chani was wooed with funny stories and lovely words, courted with intense looks and glances, and treated to new visions of herself.

Back home in Kuala Lumpur, no one quite noticed the new flush on Chani's face. Prem came to her house the next day. It was

---

3   Traditional attire with fitted trousers worn by Indian women.

mid-morning. He walked right to the back of the house to greet and embrace Chani's mother who was busy with chores.

"You must have lunch," said Chani's mother.

And so Chani spent yet another day glowing as Prem watched her every move. Her fingers smouldered when she washed the rice as Prem stood next to her by the kitchen sink. The back of her neck tingled as she stirred dhal on the stove while sensing Prem's gaze upon it. Lunch was soon over. Prem said, "*Sat shri akal*,"[4] Chani's mother embraced him and wished him well. He said a little "bye" to Chani and left.

That evening, the phone rang. Chani raced for it. She knew it was for her. "I have fallen in love with you. I leave for London tomorrow morning. I will write to you," he said. Chani's head was a blur as her heart raced. She said nothing except for a quiet "bye".

For days, Chani kept her eyes on the post box. Then one day it arrived, a blue aerogramme post-marked United Kingdom. She folded it up matchbox size and slipped it into her brassiere. She was on her way upstairs when her mother called her to collect the laundry from the clothes line. She could almost hear her heart beating against the folded-up aerogramme nestled against her, as she squinted against the afternoon sun in the backyard. She dumped the clothes on the table and ran upstairs, locked her door and read and reread her first love letter.

She wrote back, requesting Prem to write to a girlfriend's address in the future. Thence ensued a poetic correspondence between Chani and Prem, and she lived from letter to letter, reading and rereading each one as if her life depended on it, sometimes in the bathroom seated in a dry corner, when she could not get her little brother to leave her room.

---

4 A traditional customary greeting between Sikhs.

Some weeks went by. In April, the HSC results were out. As expected, Chani did well and a couple of weeks later came the news of an offer from the Faculty of Arts, University of Malaya, and also from the Faculty of Law, University of Singapore. Singapore was too far away, it was decided. So University of Malaya it was to be. Chani, as was custom, did not raise any issue. She never did.

One day, Nice Uncle and Modern Aunt decided to take her with them on a holiday to Hunter Uncle's house, as a treat for her excellent results. Chani was excited to be with her cousins again. They sat up nights listening to the poetic contents of Prem's letters.

One evening, the older girls were taking a long walk with Modern Aunt, who wore skirts and capris more than traditional Punjabi clothing. Unlike their mothers, she was a working lady, bearing promise of the new and the unventured. She talked to them about being girls. "This is the time when you will start to be interested in boys, but you should be careful. You can talk to me, I will understand," she said. Modern Aunt knew everything, she said it would be OK. And so … Chani told her, about the letters, the poems, the smiles and the laughs. Chani told her about how he made her feel pretty, as she remembered how she smiled at herself in the mirror, feeling like the beautiful Mumtaz in Hindi films. Her gaggle of cousins, hearts swelling, lilting, laughing, teasing as Chani told her story of Prem. Gosh, even his name meant "love". Modern Aunt listened and smiled. Chani slept well that night, smiling in her sleep. Telling Modern Aunt had made her lighter of head and heart.

She had no idea what the next morning would bring.

Chani bounded into the breakfast room, and suddenly the chatter was hushed. Her cousins hurried out of the room and the womenfolk receded into the background. Modern Aunt stood her ground, watching Chani intently. Hunter Uncle appeared, sitting stern at the breakfast table. He was seated at the head of the table with the other elders standing around him. Parathas, toast and marmalade remained untouched on the table. Once-hot tea was slowly turning tepid.

"So you want to marry your cousin-brother, is it?" It was as if Hunter Uncle had thrown a stone at her. Marriage? The thought had not even crossed Chani's mind. What was Hunter Uncle even talking about! It had not occurred to Chani that Prem was a cousin-brother, not even a cousin, and definitely not a brother … well, certainly not by blood. She dwelt on that for a moment until her thoughts forced her to look at Modern Aunt, standing tall, a bit arrogant. But when their eyes met, momentarily, Modern Aunt dipped her eyes, averting from the betrayal she could see in Chani's eyes. Hunter Uncle hurled insult after insult at Chani, shrivelling her up inside, causing her to miss the big bear-ness of her own father and his genteel gregariousness. He would never have shouted at her in this way, as if she had sullied anything – virtue, purity or family.

That very afternoon, Chani was taken back to Kuala Lumpur by two other uncles and the modern, young aunt. She sat cold and cut-off through the whole car ride whilst the uncles and aunt chatted over her head about family politics.

Once back home, she was summoned to the living room as soon as all the elders had been informed of what had transpired. Chani said that she liked Prem. Her father seemed a little shaken at her declaration whilst her mother met that rebellion with a tight slap. When her family, all of them, told her the liaison could not happen, Chani cried as though her heart would break. Modern Aunt took her upstairs to her bedroom, got her to bathe and gave her a little pill. "This will make you feel better," she said. Chani looked at her with hurt and question, and she responded as she always did, with a look of the unsaid adage "… it's for your own good." When Chani recounted the events later, she thought maybe Modern Aunt herself had been told the same thing before, because of the smirk that curved her lips. Chani continued to cry quietly but eventually fell asleep.

She learnt later that her elders had gone to Prem's brother's house that very evening, laid their turbans at his feet and asked forgiveness for their daughter's doing. They requested firmly but politely that Prem should have no dealings with Chani. Intra-family liaisons were not accepted in traditional Sikh families. Even though Prem was related to Chani's family only through marriage and not by any blood line, he was not acceptable to Chani's family. There was already existing distrust of Prem's family by Chani's elders, following the marriage of Hunter Uncle into Prem's family. There were even some allegations of black magic practice in Prem's family.

A week later, Chani was told that she would not be allowed to go out on her own anywhere, and that she would not go to university that year. Chani did not react to the edict. She continued to live in her dream world of Prem, Hindi songs and storybooks for some weeks. Then May 13th[5] struck and a curfew was imposed. The whole country was topsy-turvy, some parts of it on fire. For Chani, the reality of May 13th was remote. There were some killings between the Malays and Chinese, she gathered, and there was nothing but that news on television. There were loads of canned food at home and she learned to like cheese sandwiches. As the pile of letters from England accumulated at her girlfriend's house, Prem became a little faraway but not forgotten.

---

5   Known as the May 13th Incident, when riots broke out in Kuala Lumpur on 13 May 1969 after the 1969 Malaysian general election, resulting in the declaration of a state of national emergency.

When May turned into June, the country settled into recognising a racialised status quo and Chani slowly awoke from her stupor. There was a letter in the mail informing her about University Malaya Orientation Week. Chani was starting to miss her school friends. *They must all be in University now*, she thought. She felt vacant. Thoughts of Prem and Hindi songs seemed insufficient.

So one June day, summoning the spirit she knew she had, she wrote a letter to her elders, imploring them to allow her to go to university. "It is not fair that I should not be allowed to continue with my education," she wrote. A few days later, the Patriarch Uncle of the family returned home at midday, contrary to routine. He summoned Chani to the living room and said, "So you want to study?"

"Yes," she answered.

"Okay, you can go to university, but you will first sign a promissory note that says you will not be in any kind of contact with that fellow in England, or have anything to do with any other fellow for that matter," Patriarch Uncle declared. Chani nodded in agreement, brow furrowed.

She signed a typed-out contract agreement. She even smiled at the irony of the importance that letters and words had for her family. Her father took her to the administration building of University Malaya to register, whilst Patriarch Uncle telephoned his professor buddies to ensure that Chani's late entry did not encounter any obstacles. Her father smiled as he watched his daughter walk toward her future. This is the right sort of future, he thought to himself.

Chani had missed Orientation Week, and even two weeks of lectures, but her friends from school filled in the blanks. Chani entered a new world, a new universe of a personal solo sojourn, and the discovery of her mind as she entered the Regency era of Jane Austen, the searching mind of TS Eliot and VS Naipaul's questioning of traditional family order. A world beyond, bigger and far more meaningful than the escape of Hindi films and extended family socials.

She even ventured into exploring the curls of the Italian language, the ancientness of Sanskrit and the cadence of the Thirukkural. The Arts Concourse was a platform for all things new, of long discussions on the meaning of life, raging Malaysian politics, the allegory of the great writers. And on some days, she would just sit alone and stare into space, thinking about who or what would happen next – remembering the cool sands of the Kampar house and how far away all that seemed.

Eventually, she collected her pile of letters from her girlfriend's house and finally wrote to Prem, telling him about all the tumultuous events of the past weeks. Prem continued to write. Once, he even sent Chani a record in the post – "The Shadow of Your Smile" along with a simple ring. Chani wrote … sometimes.

She was caught up with campus life, dressing up daily, un-uniformed, sometimes in vogue in stylish bell bottoms, at times also in crisp cotton sarees or chic *churidar* suits, in her element with her gang of girls and boys. She started to have friends who were boys – studious boys who copied her lecture notes, serious boys who secretly admired her, boisterous boys who teased and some nice chaps she talked to about life. Her days were full with lectures, assignments and readings. Life became less imagined and far more real. Chani was getting to know herself, the outreach of her own mind, as she read, reflected and debated writings by literary greats, even as she revelled in coffee and talk, and interacted with other young evolving minds, some staid, some revolutionary, others just revolting, yet some just wonderfully engaging.

She could not remember when or why she stopped writing to Prem.

Author's Note

My first draft of this story was written sometime during the 1990s, when my children were in their teens and I had some time to reflect on life. I remember writing snippets of the story on a pack of note cards. As pieces of memory flashed in my mind's eye, I created narrative links and dwelled over poetic, lyrical words to express sentiments, thus embellishing simple life activities and happenings with fragments of ethos and nostalgia.

I believe most fiction writing is rooted in personal history. There are moments of pain, pleasure, even mere words that some of us inexplicably relive over and over again. I remember writing elsewhere that writing is an act of courage to share, in an attempt to come to terms with insecurities, uncertainties, perplexities and truths. Many writers would have started out scribbling notes to liberate personal tensions, anxieties and hurts. The deepest notes in much fiction writing are arguably personal.

It is my personal maxim that writing has to be simple and honest – simple so as to be accessible and honest as based on the truth of experience and/or feeling.

Children's Day

Charlotte Hammond

Children's Day is a contemporary popular holiday in South Korea today. It was promoted by social activists in the mid-20th century to elevate the status of children in society. Today, parents celebrate their children on this day much in the way that children celebrate their parents on Mother's Day and Father's Day.

Ancestor worship has long been practiced throughout East Asia, yet, among the younger generations of South Koreans, it is – like Buddhism, shamanism and other practices that have characterised Korean life prior to the Korean War (and Westernisation) – becoming less popular. Traditionally, the oldest men in the family performed the *jesa* ceremony.[1] Married Korean women attend *jesa* ceremonies devoted to their husband's ancestors. The rituals include an elaborate preparation of food, assembling of an altar to commemorate the departed and the donning of traditional clothes.

When I board the coach bus to Seoul, I'm happy to see that it's nearly empty, as it is every year. Most people don't take bus trips on Children's Day. If they do, it's to Everland or a leisure resort that caters to parents with children, somewhere for a joyful outing, a photogenic place to make memories. I wonder if any other grown children travel to visit their parents for Children's Day. If they're out there, cradling a homecoming gift like it's *Chuseok*,[2] I hope they're heading toward a happier destination.

At the back of the bus, a college couple don matching T-shirts, headphones and drawn faces. Like me, they're too old for this holiday. An old woman plays Candy Crush in the very first seat, her face twisted with age and concentration like a knot of garlic. No

---

1 A memorial to honour ancestors and departed family members.
2 A major harvest festival, celebrated in both North and South Korea.

doubt grandchildren await her in some Seoul apartment complex, expecting gifts or, at the very least, her homemade sweets.

Given the choice, I wouldn't spend a beautiful June weekend in my parents' airless apartment in Northwest Seoul, sweating and cooking, and dwelling on the past. But each year, I book my bus ticket ahead of time, like you would for a major national holiday. I purchase an assortment of expensive fruits and maybe a few bottles of Namhae *makgeolli*[3] for my father, pack a small bag and prepare to endure the weekend ahead.

There's plenty of room in the overhead shelf to fit my tray of "local peaches" bought at the Hyundai Department store. My mother requests them every year, not that she or my father enjoy them. They'll sit in a ceremonial stack, an offering of remembrance, until they cave in on themselves with overripe neglect and have to be thrown away.

A text comes in from my mother as the bus mounts the highway. "When are you getting here? I already started cooking. I wish you had come a day earlier." This year, I started a new job managing a local hotel. Nothing my parents would brag about, if they did that type of thing, but it's a good job. I'm trying to hang on to it. Weekends and holidays aren't exactly the easiest time to ask for time off in the tourism industry. My parents have not asked about my new job, and I wonder if I'll have the courage to tell them about it tonight.

In another text message, one between both of my parents and me, my father sends through a few photographs. Taking pictures was one thing he used to enjoy when my brother and I were young. My parents' home and digital devices are filled with photos from before; none of us have many photos of the three of us after. "New Photo Message (4)", my phone reads, and I'm tempted to switch it off.

---

3 Unfiltered rice wine.

I open the photos anyway. The first is of a slack-jawed baby in pyjamas, staring up at the camera from a recognisable floor from my past. In the next photo, there are two boys standing beside each other. The older boy is in a school uniform and the younger, still too young for school, holds a giant plastic yellow backpack. My first day of public school. We have identical haircuts with thick bangs. Another image: my mother holds my brother beside a jungle gym that stood outside of the Seoul apartment where they still live.

My father doesn't frame these photos with anything other than the date of my brother's disappearance. I was 12 years old. It has been over a decade. I wonder what my parents feel when they look at these photos now. Do they make them feel better? Or worse?

When I look at pictures of Jae-won, I go back and forth between the two of us. I study our faces, noticing how we look the same, yet different. This preoccupies me more than the unanswered questions, the length of time. Are our similarities preserved outside of these photographs? How the shape of our cheeks are curved in a similar, but unique way. How he disappeared, and I have grown up. How he occupies a place in my family's life that is unchanged, in a way, immortal. And as for me? What is my place? What has my life become?

My brother didn't disappear exactly on Children's Day that year, but it was the same weekend, and so the holiday has become, both practically and symbolically, the end of Jae-won's life and forever the day of his *gije*,[4] when we honour him and mourn the day everything changed.

I doubt that I will ever get married and have children, but if I do, I plan to celebrate a different kind of Children's Day. Not too long ago, I read about how more and more wealthy Korean parents have begun taking their children on holiday for

---

4 Death anniversary.

Children's Day, to child-friendly resorts in the mountains or to the beaches of Guam. I could co-opt this idea, I think, as I watch the scenery of the middle provinces whip by. Instead of a typical family vacation though, we would wander away from Children's Day and see pieces of the world outside. We could ride street cars in San Francisco or watch the sun come up over the immense mountains of Nepal. Our tradition could be a day that emphasises the beauty of the present over the past.

I've never left Korea, and neither have my parents. After Jae-won disappeared, I used to beg them for a trip abroad. Perhaps if we travelled to the right place, we might see him walking down the street with a new family, and we'd be able to spirit him home. I told myself I wanted to travel to look for Jae-won, but I know I really wanted to escape. To be immersed in any scenery other than my parents' home and its static misery.

The last time I asked my father for a trip was on a rare outing to have ice cold noodles at a small restaurant near our house. At that time, Jae-won had been gone almost a year; spring and cherry blossoms and the light weather of hope were just around the corner.

"Please, *Appa*,"[5] I said, swirling the remaining tendrils of grey noodles in their vinegary lagoon of cool broth. "All my classmates are taking trips these days. We could go to the Philippines and learn how to snorkel!"

The table was quiet for a few seconds before my father reached across the table to slap me across the face. My mother gasped with surprise, but did not say anything.

"How can you think such a stupid thing, Jae-yoo? Of course, we're not going to leave Korea. We can't leave Korea – we can't leave this neighbourhood! Not now, not ever. What if your brother comes back looking for us?"

---

5   Dad in Korean.

* * *

The air at Express Bus Terminal in Seoul is clear and warm; it is close to evening but the sky is still bright. A rare city day without any smog.

As kids, Jae-won and I were allowed to play just about anywhere we wanted in our neighbourhood. You didn't have to go too far to get to a stretch of emptiness, it was an up-and-coming place to live back then, with a lot of construction. In fact, that was what the police suspected at first: either my brother had been wandering around a construction site and got trapped or buried by accident, or that some itinerant worker – a foreign worker, many suspected – had taken Jae-won for any number of terrible reasons.

Now, the neighbourhood is far from new and improving. The buildings are squat and beige, resembling tightly packed boxes on a forgotten storeroom shelf.

Dim light greets me inside my childhood home. The heavy, hot air seems to close around my throat, and the *jesa* altar to Jae-won is half set up with his school photographs, fake flowers and the paper screen behind it all. A single fan blows a warmish feeling of relief around the front room where I set down my duffle bag. There, on the old white sofa stained with time and indifference, my father sits holding a shallow cup of cool barley tea.

"It's been a long time, *Appa*," and I bow to him formally, for my small and serious father's presence always demands some level of deference.

My father forces a smile. "Your mother will be glad you're here, Jae-yoo." I nearly blush at the uncommon sound of my father saying my name.

"It's very hot out," I say in his direction without looking at him, and flap my polo shirt away from my damp back. "Is there more barley tea?"

He motions me toward the kitchen. I place the tray of fruit on the altar, looking down at the perfect pink and white shapes that glisten from the heat of the journey.

"*Ya*, don't put them there in the box they came in! Here, watch out, I have a plate for them." It was my mother, a moving streak of cooking smells and shuffling feet, not wanting her son's altar smeared by my laziness.

In college, when I had a few friends, almost none of them practiced *jesa* anymore. Most came from Christian families who went to church on occasion, or they came from families without religion and the old traditions had faded away. In fact, this practice is not only a habit that anchors my family to the absence of my brother, but it is also the last relic of my mother's Buddhist faith. *Jesa* is now the only time that her devoted character gets a chance to shine. I let her set up the fruit on a traditional platter while I fish through the refrigerator for the cool comfort of barley tea.

"Now that you're here, we can begin frying the *jeon*,"[6] my mother says, and points to the group of bowls cluttering the stove, where a shallow frying pan with a pool of yellow cooking oil stands waiting. My mother always wants to fry the *jeon* with me, even though most mothers wouldn't dare let their eldest unmarried sons into the kitchen.

"Ah, Jae-won especially loved the squash *jeon*. And he could really eat a lot," she says with pride in her voice, a serene look casting over her worn face as she turns on the burner to heat the frying oil.

The Saturday of my brother's disappearance, my mother was at the temple, early. This wasn't out of the ordinary, she was always there those mornings. It was also the last morning she would ever spend there, washing one hand at a time with cold water, and praying in uninterrupted silence. The mountains

---

6   A savoury pancake featuring a range of fillings such as meat, vegetables, potatoes or seafood.

before her, the ocean at her back. I can picture her tiny figure seated and focused, content in her prayer and meditation. Now, looking back, I understand that going to the temple was as much a spiritual cleansing as it was a precious moment to herself, away from a demanding household where her two boys ran wild and her husband preoccupied himself with the Doosan Bears game.

During those days, I had started cooking in the mornings when my mother was at the temple. That Saturday, I made Jae-won and myself fried eggs. The oil poured out too fast into the pan, the eggs tasted soggy and I remember Jae-won complained and made himself instant noodles instead. Frustrated, I left without him. He was still in his cartoon character pyjamas and I heard him call my name as I descended the stairs of our building.

Boys from my neighbourhood, and a few girls too, used to meet on a dirt-covered hill behind one of the construction sites for a new multi-use building.

Before we broke into our games, I got the attention of Ki-yeon, a girl who often played in the group. At that time in my life, Ki-yeon had my eye. One day of play, and I started to take notice of her delicate cheeks and smooth, pale limbs, the perfect movement of her hair.

That Saturday morning, we avoided eye contact as we talked. We focused on kicking small clumps of dirt or rock down the dusty hill so that they rolled into the construction site. All of us kids were kicking and scuffing the ground – our expensive sneakers be damned – when Ki-yeon asked me if I had ever been to the United States. Seconds after Ki-yeon asked me this question, her bright eyes peeking out from under her bangs, I heard my brother's voice.

He cursed my name in a little-kid way. Blocking out the sound of Jae-won calling me a dirty slug and an ugly turd, I told Ki-yeon no, I had never been to the United States. Why? Before the out-of-breath and furious Jae-won had gotten far enough up the hill to yank on my sleeve and rap me on the arm, Ki-yeon told me that she and her parents were moving there that summer. And she was nervous. I was shocked. Ki-yeon's news struck a blow to the centre of my body just seconds before my brother's little fist jabbed my arm, and then my shoulder. I turned away from my crush to shove my brother with force and the other kids cried out in giddy laughter as Jae-won, red-faced, stumbled on the incline of the hill and fell.

Before Jae-won could retaliate, one of the boys in the neighbourhood, probably the oldest one there, suggested we all play manhunt, and he put out his fist for rock-paper-scissors, to see who would be the seeker.

To my disappointment, I was chosen as the seeker. I would have tried to hide with Ki-yeon and asked her more questions – when she would leave, how long she would stay, if her parents would take her to Disney World and New York City.

The kids on the hill began to scatter before I closed my eyes.

Im Min-jae, the older boy who decided we should play manhunt, was the last person to see my brother. He saw him go away from the construction side, crossing the hill, toward a cluster of wisteria bushes that were, at the time, still half in bloom, the papery pastel blossoms scattering the ground.

Before dusk, the neighbourhood kids' game of manhunt became a true manhunt, with parents beginning the search and the police showing up not long after that. All of us kids were separated and questioned. I was afraid to tell the officers that my brother and I had argued a little bit, but I told them anyway, because I had so little else to tell. Everyone wanted answers from everyone there, but especially from me, and I had none to give.

The adults were maddened by our lack of information. The truth was unsatisfactory, but nothing out of the ordinary happened that day.

Did we usually hide in the construction sites? Yes, sometimes. Did we ever see anyone or anything unusual when we did so? No, they were nearly always empty; sometimes Min-jae would dare us to drink from a soju bottle if one was left behind. We saw remnants of the workers: extinguished cigarette butts, crumpled receipts from convenience stores, a broken pair of protective glasses. If any worker was on the job, we wouldn't hide there. It was the emptiness that drew us there, not any kind of mystery or danger.

One boy claimed he saw a foreign man standing outside the construction site wearing a raincoat. When the police asked what kind of foreigner, the boy said "white". Im Min-jae also told police in an interview that he thought he had seen the raincoat man before, but was unable to provide more details or identify him from a police sketch.

The next day, the police found Jae-won's set of house keys about 100 metres from the wisteria bushes, close to another partially occupied apartment complex. Shoe prints matching the sneakers my brother wore that day were also found around the wisteria bush and the other apartment complex. And then the search for Jae-won went cold.

My mother and I begin to fry the *jeon*. It is my job to make sure the oil doesn't get too hot and decide when each piece has to be flipped. Sweat pours out of each crevice of my body as I listen to my mother discuss one of her favourite memories, which was when she brought in homemade food for Jae-won's classmates on his birthday.

"Your brother's eyes were so wide when I opened up the Tupperware of the *tteokbokki*[7] in front of everyone, and his teacher

---

7   Korean rice cakes stir fried in a sweet and spicy sauce.

told me it looked even better than the kind at her favourite *pocha*.[8]
And then, of course, everyone wanted to sit next to your brother
during the birthday meal. He was always very popular in school
…"

The funny thing about my mother's story is that I always
remember my brother being something of a picky eater. I had
always liked my mother's *jeon* at holiday meals. Jae-won's altar
pancakes year after year had kind of ruined them for me, but
I used to eat them until I got sick at most family meals, while
Jae-won would pick at his rice and wait for the sweets afterward.
Noodles, though, he always loved noodles. He liked western food,
too. He'd always put a slice of cheese into his *ramyeon*,[9] like he did
the last day we had breakfast together. Spaghetti or *ramyeon* or ice-
cold buckwheat noodles, my brother would delight in anything he
could slurp.

My father crosses through the kitchen behind me, muttering a
baseball chant under his breath.

"You know," my father says loudly, and it is clear he is
addressing me. "I ran into Im Min-jae's father at the corner mart
this week. He's just finished his law degree at Seoul National
University, can you believe it? A neighbourhood success story!"
My father exclaims, showing a rare glimmer of true delight. My
mother makes a noise in agreement.

"How many dangerous criminals he will be able to put away. Im
Min-jae really was always a promising boy." Even though the lead
of the foreigner in the raincoat had not panned out, my parents
somehow considered Min-jae a hero in their son's disappearance
for having come up with a lead. Aside from recounting what my
brother ate for breakfast, I had not been able to help with the
investigation.

---

8 Korean hot snack food stand.
9 Korean instant noodles.

"I'm going to take a cold shower before we eat. I'll dress nicely in Jae-won's memory."

I turn the nozzle to cold, open my mouth and let the cold water pour in, and pretend I am opening my mouth to let out a scream. How many more weekends, how many more Children's Days do I have to spend like this? Reliving the same day, the same stale memories of my brother over and over; marking time, edging closer and closer to whatever dark hole in the Earth had swallowed my brother and kept him for good?

After putting on a fresh polo shirt and pair of light pants, we sit down to eat. The smells of cooked rice, beef, fish and *songpyeon*[10] fills the air, and my heart sinks a little when I see the bowl of piping hot rice on Jae-won's altar. My mother always uses a plastic bowl featuring a cartoon character – its colourful expression faded with time – that belonged to my brother.

It is difficult to concentrate on anything as my father calls for my brother's spirit. The apartment is still stiflingly hot though it is nearly dark outside, and the candle my mother has lit in my brother's honour seems like more of a reminder of the physical discomfort in the room than a beckoning for Jae-won's long-lost presence. I imagine how Jae-won would handle this repeated misery if he were here. It's impossible for me to imagine him as an adult, so I imagine him here as a child, tugging at my clothes and looking at the food on our table with disgust, whispering in my ear that he'd rather go make some instant noodles.

"Jae-yoo, *ya*," my mother raps my shoulder and motions for me to get up. It's my turn, the eldest son, to contribute *sapsi*[11] to my brother's altar. I pierce the mound of rice in the Pororo bowl with a metal spoon, careful to keep it balanced upright, as the plastic bowl is wobbly; I've learned from past mistakes.

---

10 Small, half-moon shaped rice cakes with sweet fillings, traditionally eaten during Chuseok.
11 A ritual that is part of the *jesa* rites of serving food to the departed at the memorial altar.

My fresh polo is already damp; but now it's time to eat. My parents seem to get lost in the movements of the meal, the clinking of spoons against dishes, the soft noises of fish and beef pieces tearing and mixing with rice. First taking a sip of rice wine, my father looks my way.

"Your mother said you were late coming down because of work." My father speaks to me in an adult voice, which should make me feel respected, but instead I feel like a new employee out to dinner with his boss.

"It's hard to get away for a long time at this time of the year. The hotel is nearly full every weekend." I realise my father hasn't actually asked a question, but I continue. "They need me there. The staff. It gets quite busy."

Another sip of his wine. My mother peeks up from her bowl of rice and continues to eat. I have hardly touched my food.

"What kind of people stay at your hotel?" His eyes narrow, but his face is unchanged.

"All kinds of people." I punch each word I speak with an anger I no longer care to contain. What kind of question is this? I have sent my parents links to the hotel website. They know I live in a popular beach town, even though they have never bothered to visit.

"Families, mostly." I add. "Young families with kids. Older couples, too. *Eomma*[12] would like the hotel. The restaurants around it are good, too. You should come down to see it sometime."

"Mmm," my father says, and picks at the pile of pancakes with his chopsticks.

"I could make a reservation for you. Even apply the employee discount. It's a nice place to go in the summertime. To cool off, you know." My mother chews her food, her eyes fixed on my father.

---

12 Mum in Korean.

"That sounds nice, Jae-yoo. Unfortunately, we aren't the kind of family that can take frivolous trips. I'm sure it's a very nice place to work." My father's voice is cool and even, and it sends a sharp wave of anger down my back. I drop my chopsticks.

"Jae-yoo, *ya*," my mother exclaims, her voice high and nervous. "You haven't eaten anything! Do you not like my cooking all of a sudden?" Her eyes are wide with hurt. The look on her face doesn't move me, and I push back from the table. Jae-won isn't here and I don't need to suffer my parents' tradition for him anymore.

"*Eomma*, I'm not hungry right now. I'm sorry. I'm stepping out for some air." I ignore my mother's pleas and do not bother to look at my father's sour face as I walk out of the apartment and into the neighbourhood.

My feet carry me in the direction of the hill, toward the place where the wisteria bushes used to grow, to the structure that now stands where our favourite construction site had been. An ordinary multi-use building. Walking inside, the building's beige entrance is already showing signs of age; the overhead lights are dim, the stairs to the first floor, which holds a dentist's office and a stationery store, are scuffed and show dirty footprints.

The second floor, I can see on the building's modest directory, houses a restaurant. Maybe I could sit there for a while to cool off. The sign reads: "Eatery: Simple Food for Wellbeing" in traditional Korean font made to look like wood carving.

A young woman with a calm, sincere-looking smile on her face tells me I can sit anywhere and asks me if I want cold or hot water to drink. Something makes me linger on her face; she is pretty and the calm tone of her voice is as soothing as a sea breeze after the day I've had.

When she brings me my cold metal cup of water, I realise she looks familiar. My insides somersault and I nearly cry out, "Son Ki-yeon?"

The woman's face reflects many of Ki-yeon's girlish features; her delicate cheeks and bright eyes. Instead of bangs, the woman wears her hair in a braid; but without a doubt, the waitress looks like the Son Ki-yeon I once knew. Would Ki-yeon really have come back from America to work here, at this small restaurant in the neighbourhood? It is easier to imagine that she turned out like Min-jae or one of the others and has moved on to a noble career. Probably, the true Ki-yeon would be unrecognisable to me now, and this waitress is a hopeful mirage. In fact, it gives me more comfort to imagine that Ki-yeon has left this place, the site of my brother's disappearance, and never returned.

The menu on the wall is written in the same carved-style font, almost made to look like a mountain-top restaurant in the countryside – it is the type of gimmick many restaurants in the area I now live in adopt to appeal to tourists. Remembering the dinner I have walked out on, I want something light and cool. Scanning the simple, meatless menu, I settle on cold noodles in a creamy sesame broth.

Jae-won would probably never have eaten this type of noodles, but they are noodles nonetheless. While I wait for Ki-yeon's adult twin to return with my order, I lose myself for a moment in a picture on the wall. A common traditional painting: mountains beside the sea, a small Buddhist temple perched in between them. There is a calmness in this painting, a calmness in this simple restaurant that sits in the place of the empty construction site where we played and played until we lost my brother and lost our childhood. It feels good to be here, alone, with things that don't belong to Children's Day, to begin something new, something peaceful, something mine.

Not-Ki-yeon sets down my bowl of noodles with a few side dishes, and another plate that holds a hardboiled egg, cut in half.

I look up at her, and consider asking her about herself. Sharing this day with a stranger, somehow, even if only for a moment.

"Some of our customers like the egg on top of the noodles, and some like it separate, so we tend to serve it separately, so you can choose how you would like to eat it. I hope you eat well," she says, her voice like gentle waves breaking on the seashore.

"Oh, that's good. Thank you."

The egg halves are alike yet not alike; one dented and one smooth, one looks somehow plumper and brighter than the other half. I pick each of them up, one at a time and submerge them in the white ocean of the cold sesame broth, and fold them into the tangle of noodles underneath.

Author's Note

While living in South Korea in my 20s, I learned about ancestor worship from a fellow female co-worker. She was a glamorous dresser with a trendy Western hairstyle. She explained the elaborate traditional meal she would prepare over the weekend with her parents, intended to honour departed relatives and ancestors she hardly knew. She spoke of her plans with a mixture of reverence and detachment. She seemed proud of the lush spread her parents would prepare, but she also sighed as she finished explaining the rituals. As with all long-held traditions, tedium is often attached.

I centred "Children's Day" around how traditions fade or live on and take new shape – either because of changes in culture or on a personal level, because the traditions are complicated or changed by events in our lives or beliefs we form as we come of age and mature. I thought it would be interesting for my main male character to help his mother with the preparation of food. This, too, combines tradition (the making of pancakes for a significant meal) with a reversal of traditional gender norms (a man helping his mother in the kitchen).

Sense of place is key to the story and I included details that underscore the main character's mood and the change he's lived through. The apartment is stagnant in time and in temperature, with the heat amplifying the main character's discomfort in his childhood home when he's tried his best to make a new life elsewhere. Inside, the home he grew up in is the same, outside time has had its way with the neighbourhood where the narrator came of age and where his brother vanished. Traditions, along with people and places, grow and change and even disappear whether or not we are ready.

Swimming

Muthusamy Pon Ramiah

In the 1950s and 1960s, the socio-economic background of some working-class families in Malaysia meant that children hardly had any coins in their pockets. Children played seasonal games throughout the year. Flying kites, shooting marbles, spinning tops, collecting empty cigarette packets, bottle caps and swimming in ponds, flooded pits and streams. The bigger boys who knew a little swimming went to the old mining pools and the brick factory where clay had been dug out, leaving deep pools of water. Almost all boys played football. They kicked around pomelos wrapped in old newspapers, tied in place with gunny strings. The boys also raided fruit orchards, mostly for guava, rambutan and mangosteen.

Besides playing these games, the boys also went looking for firewood in the nearby rubber estate and took the opportunity of playing in any pit of water and collected rubber seeds scattered under the trees for their sisters to play girls' games like hopscotch.

Very few houses had radios. The programmes on Radio Malaya, which included Singapore, broadcasted for about 45 minutes in the morning, another 45 minutes in the afternoon and an hour and a half in the evening. The children of that generation only heard of something called television in the USA and England, and dreamed about a time when it would come to their country.

It was after lunchtime. Raju was getting restless, standing on the veranda, looking at the sky, the sun blazing, the wind-combed clouds hanging low, their underbellies a little grey. Walking in and out, and looking at the road. In the morning, his mother had said it had rained heavily in the night. She didn't call it the monsoon rain. For her, it was Deepavali rain because it started in mid-October and carried on until early January. He had slept through the rain.

He sat on the rattan chair, sliding down to a reclining position, browsing through the pictures in the old cinema magazine, absentmindedly. He had looked at the pictures of the actors and actresses many times. Now there was nothing new to look at. He had read the short story in the magazine once and didn't want to look at it again. The writer had used a lot of long, unfamiliar words. He didn't have a dictionary to look up their meanings. And he was not in the mood. School holidays were not for looking at all that. He was bored.

He thought of Lim, his classmate. Lim's father worked in a bank. He used to take him to his club for swimming during the weekends. Lim talked a lot about the club, the long swimming pool with the clean blue water, the lifeguard and the variety of food and drinks there. That school holiday, Lim had gone to Singapore with his family. His grandparents, on his mother's side, lived there. They went by the night mail, sleeping in the berths. In Singapore, they would be going to the Tiger Balm Garden and visiting Sentosa Island, riding on the new cable car and sightseeing, and eating at different foodcourts and restaurants every day. Singapore sounded like a faraway country.

He wished his parents would take him and Kamala somewhere for the holidays. It was so difficult sitting in the house and looking at the walls. His mother only switched on the small transistor radio when the Tamil programmes came on in the morning, afternoon and evening, and then switched it off to save electricity. Now he could only think of Samad and his friends out there, somewhere. Samad had promised to take him swimming that afternoon, but he didn't say where.

His mother came in from the kitchen after washing up the plates and glasses, and making sure the aluminium kitchen sink was spotless.

"Leave that magazine alone and do your homework. How many times do you want to look at the pictures?"

Always read your books, do your homework, he thought, as he looked up at her.

"Ma, there is no homework, Ma. This is December school holidays. I will study after we buy the new books in January. There is still three weeks to go," Raju said, shaking his legs.

"Stop shaking your legs! Such a bad habit!"

Raju stopped his legs from shaking. He didn't shake them. They shook by themselves.

"I know it is school holidays but that doesn't mean you shouldn't touch the books. Practice your arithmetic, memorise the times tables, learn some new words every day. Remember, next year you are going to standard six. Very important year. You must pass the government examination if you want to go on to Form One."

"I know, Ma. How many times must you tell me? Telling the same thing again and again!"

"Why would I tell you so many times if you spent a little time studying every day? You only look at the magazines and the comic books or go out and play with the boys. Learn something. It will be helpful next year," she said and went into the bedroom.

His father was already taking a nap. He worked the evening shift that week. Kamala was in the bedroom, lying on her stomach, drawing. She liked to draw the matchstick man and his matchstick wife in their home, on the beach, under the trees and so on, filling up the drawing pad. He went into the bedroom and took out the old exercise book from the rack on the wall.

"Memorise two-times table to twelve-times table. I will ask you to recite them in the evening. After that, if you feel sleepy, sleep. Don't go out in the hot sun," his mother whispered, looking at his father who was sleeping on his side on the mat. *My family is poor compared to Lim's*, Raju thought.

He went back to the front room and stared at the times table at the bottom of the exercise book back cover. The small print always made him unhappy. He slid down the chair lazily, knitted his brows and went through the nine-times table. He closed his eyes and repeated it but got stuck halfway. He looked through the table again, closed his eyes and tried once more. This time, he got through it without a hitch. He skipped the ten-times table. It was like *kacang putih*[1] for him. So easy. All he had to do was go from one to 12, adding a zero at the end of each number. As he started on the eleven-times table, he heard a forced whistling, more air than sound, followed by "*Swin, swin, swin.*"[2]

He put the exercise book down on the table and listened without moving. *Swin, swin.* He looked at the bedroom door. All was silent there. He tiptoed to the verandah and looked out. There was no one on the road or behind the bougainvillea bush. He tiptoed to the back and opened the back door. Jambu was standing behind the murungai tree,[3] half hidden.

"All are waiting at the railway gate! Somebody must come to your house and call you, *ah*? Come, come!"

"Shhhh! Don't make noise. Wait, I will come. My slippers are in front."

"I give you one *nimit*.[4] If you don't come in one *nimit*, I will go away. If I don't go back quickly, they will leave me and go, all because of you!" Jambu said, impatiently.

---

1 Literal reference to roasted or fried nuts (a snack), also a slang meaning simple or easy.

2 Swim.

3 Moringa or drumstrick tree.

4 Minute.

"I am coming. You wait here."

Raju latched the back door, tiptoed out, closed the front door noiselessly and left, half running around the block.

* * *

"You said you wanted to swim," Samad said. "All the time you tell me about your school friend who swims in the swimming pool at his father's club. So, I pity you and tell you to follow me, and see what you do? What time did I tell you to come here and what time you are coming? I must send someone to go to your house and call you?"

"Sorry. I forgot," he lied.

"This is the first and last time. Next time we won't wait!"

The other boys looked at him disapprovingly and then at Samad, who was the leader of the pack. They started walking down the railway track. Jambu and the other boys skipped over a sleeper on one leg every now and then as they walked. Samad walked on the rail, balancing himself with his hands stretched out. Not far from Bengali Kampong, he saw a boy in knee-deep grass and creepers on a slope, a little away from the railway track embankment. He was holding a sickle.

"Going to the pit?" the boy asked.

"Yes, want to come?" Samad said.

The boy slipped the sickle in amongst the creepers and joined them on the railway track. He was taller than Samad and had traces of hair on his lip and chin. He was sweating, smelling of grass.

A little further, the track took a curve and there was the pond-like stretch of water by the railway track. Raju had seen it from the train when he went to school. Not far up the slope were the cowsheds and then the rows of wooden houses with rusting tin roofs. The pool of water was shielded from the kampong by tall *lalang*[5] grass and bushes where birds perched in the shade, eating wild fruits and taking flight as the train trundled by, blowing its steam horn.

The boys began to take off their shirts and shorts. They were not wearing anything under their shorts. They rolled their clothes and placed them on the grass along with their Japanese slippers.

"What are you waiting for? Come, take off your clothes and jump in!" Samad said, standing naked. The boy who smelled of grass had hair. Raju looked down.

He looked at the stretch of water. It was like a polished mirror. The water was clean, crystal-clear. He could see the grass on the bottom and the individual *lalang* sprouting from the mud and standing above the water. A wind was blowing down the hill carrying with it the smell of cow dung, rotting wood and wet grass. The blue sky and the low, silvery clouds looked like they were inside the water.

Pinching his nose with one hand, the boy with the hair ran down the track and jumped into the water, lifting his legs and making a big splash. Samad, Jambu and the other boys whose names he didn't know followed him, making splash after splash. The water was not very deep, it just reached Samad's waist. He could see their nakedness under the water. Particles of sand-like mud rose from the bottom of the pit now. They began to splash about, going through the motions of swimming, trying to somersault, standing on their hands and falling on their backs. The water entered their noses, making them choke and cough fitfully, their eyes watering. The clear, clean water was turning into the colour of mud.

Samad noticed Raju was still standing on the track, his shirt and shorts on, watching. He beckoned him to jump in, but Raju

---

5 A type of wild grass commonly found in Malaysia.

hesitated. He had not expected *this* to be the swimming pool. Just then, the *dak dadak, dak dadak* beat of an approaching train came from the railway track. He could feel the vibration. It was the 2.45 passenger train from Klang.

The boys kept waving and calling him, telling him to take off his clothes and jump into the water. Again, Raju hesitated, shy to take off his clothes, worried about the churned, muddy water and what might be lurking there. As the vibration from the track got stronger and the *dak dadak* sound got louder, he quickly got down from the side of the track and stood in knee-deep water, holding up his shorts, a little hunched, facing away, waiting for the train to pass. As the three-coach train approached, the boys began to leap out of the water, competing with each other to show off their nakedness. The train, now slanting a little because of the curve, trundled down the track, the wheels screeching. A gust of wind moved Raju, like the train was pushing him out of its way and into the water.

After the train had passed, the boys led by Samad walked out of the water gleaming in their nakedness and caught him. The big boy with the hair stripped him and carried him on his shoulders and ran and jumped. Raju fell face down in the water. The churned water entered his nose, choking him. He sputtered, coughed and fought for breath. Samad patted him on the back until the painful fit of coughing stopped. He wanted to get out of the water but they wouldn't let him go, circling him and laughing.

The boy with the hair taught him how to take a deep breath, hold his nose and duck under water and stay there for as long as he could. He tried a few times and found it fun. Every time he opened his wet eyes, the muddy water and his friends were still there. He liked the boy for his kindness and joined in the frolicking, getting along with the group. Then the boys took turns going up the embankment of the track and running down and jumping in the water. He, too, jumped from the track, holding his nose with one hand and covering himself with the other.

The boy with the hair then went to the other side of the track and held his hands out like Superman and ran up the track and leaped into the water. The muddy water splashed on the other boys. He challenged the other boys to do the same. They went across the track and stood in single file and took their turn to do as the boy with the hair had done. While waiting his turn, Samad suddenly ran and jumped into the water. He kept looking back and ducking under the water. Raju saw a woman walking on the path by the side of the track, her head covered with her sari because of the heat. *She must have missed the train*, he thought, as he followed the other boys, running and jumping into the water.

"What to do now?" he asked, looking bewildered.

"Hide, hide, go behind the *lalang*! Go underwater," Samad said.

Pinching their noses, they all went underwater. After some time, one by one they popped their heads out of the water with their mouths open wide, gasping for air. The woman was walking opposite the pool. She didn't look at them. They sucked in air and ducked in the water again and stayed under for what felt like a long time, their lungs on the verge of exploding, crying out for air. When one by one their heads popped out of the water and they opened their eyes, the woman had gone some distance.

"My sister," Samad said, rubbing his eyes, turning them even redder.

The fun was gone for him, but the others continued to splash in the water, wrestling and throwing the fine mud at each other. Samad joined them. Raju wondered how he could be so brave and continue to play in the water after his sister had seen him naked. He sat on the edge of the water and watched them, waiting for them to get out of the muddy pool so that he could go home. The others continued playing in the water for a long time until the boy with the hair got out of the water, splashing the water on his face, wiping his hands and legs. He said he had to go back and continue cutting the grass. It was already late. The sky was getting cloudy, changing colour from silver to grey. All of them got out of the water, washing their faces, hands and legs in the clearer water by the edge of the pool, where the *lalang* stood swaying in the wind.

"Why is he cutting the grass?" Raju asked.

"To feed the cows, that's why," Jambu said. "His family has a lot of cows. His father sells milk. People also buy cow dung from them."

"Buy cow dung? For what?"

"For manure. It's good manure for vegetable plants."

Maybe that's why I hate eating vegetables, Raju thought.

"They also have rubber trees. A few acres of them. It is called a smallholding. He knows how to tap the trees. He stopped going to school after standard six. In the afternoon, he looks after the cows and cuts grass for them."

They continued to walk in silence, feeling a little tired.

"Why were you playing in the water even after your sister saw us?" Raju asked. "Not worried?"

"You see, whether I stopped straight away or swam a little more doesn't make any difference. My sister has already seen me. When I go home, my mother is going to take care of me properly. That is very sure. So, I might as well enjoy myself before the caning. I only hope my sister doesn't tell my mother," said Samad.

Raju felt better. He looked at the oil-stained railway sleepers as he walked.

"I don't worry, they won't kill us," Samad said, walking on the rail, his hand on Raju's shoulder. "They will scold us, maybe beat us a little. That's normal. They know we are young, we like to swim, play games and all. Last time, they were also young! If we don't do all this now, then when are we going to do it, after we become old? Too late by then."

"Samad, if your sister tells your mother, then your mother will tell my mother. And my mother will tell my father first thing when he returns home from work," Jambu said. "But I like to *swin!*"

Raju sighed and walked on, counting the railway sleepers. They parted company at the railway gate, going their separate ways. As he was walking up the hill, he saw Samad's mother walking down the hill.

"Raju, where is he, your friend Samad?"

"He has gone home, I think." He didn't look at her.

"You better go home straight away. Your mother is waiting for you. She is worried." She didn't smile.

* * *

At home, his mother was sitting on the rattan chair, combing Kamala's hair and braiding it. Kamala was sitting on the floor, cross-legged. There was no sign of his father. *It must be past 4 o'clock*, he thought. How time had passed. He hesitated a moment before heading for the bathroom. His mother called him. He walked back and stood at a distance.

"Come closer," she said. "Kamala, on the light."

Kamala switched on the light. His mother looked up and down at him.

"Why are your eyes so red? How did you get that mud on your eyebrows, lips, ears, hands and legs? Where did you go? I told you not to go out."

He stood kneading his hands, his mind going blank.

"Kamala, bring the cane!"

Kamala, three years younger than him, was behaving like his class monitor. She brought the cane that was inserted in the grill of the bedroom window. His mother got up, took the cane from the monitor, lunged and caught him by the hand. The grip was firm. One sharp, biting slash on his calf.

"Tell you to memorise your times tables and you quietly sneak out and go swimming! Playing in the dirty water without any clothes!"

Another slash on the shin as he started twisting in pain. Kamala was watching, bewildered, her eyes wide.

"I have been telling you not to mix with all those naughty boys, but you never listen to me. You mix with them. Play all kinds of games with them and today you went swimming with them! Will you do that again? Tell me, will you go there again?"

One more cut on the back of the knee. It stung, like the skin was splitting.

"Will you go and swim in that pit where the buffaloes used to lie down? The water is dirty with all the buffalo urine and dung!"

One more cut on the other calf.

But there was no buffalo in the water. It was so clean, so clear that he could see the grass on the floor of the pool, the *lalang* growing from the bottom. He wanted to protest but he knew it would only make things more difficult.

One double cut on the buttocks. Another one on the back of the knee, then another on his heel as he hopped on one leg.

"*Amma*,[6] don't beat *Anna*.[7] Enough, *Amma*!" cried Kamala. Tears began to gather in her eyes. She had not expected it to go that far. Their mother ignored her, waving the cane around.

"You want to get skin disease? Want to walk around smelling like a buffalo, scratching all over? You want to drown in the dirty water?"

---

6 Mother in Tamil.

7 Elder brother in Tamil.

Two successive cuts on the calves like a crescendo before the song and dance ended. She let go of his hand.

"Next time you go, I will tell *Appa*![8] He will skin you alive! Luckily for you, he has gone to work. Now go and bathe. Don't just pour water on your head and come out. I want to see all the mud and the smell of the buffalo pit scrubbed off you!"

He wiped his tears with his arm and went into the bathroom and closed the door behind him. *Buffalo pit? The boys never said anything about it or the mud on my eyebrows and my red eyes*, he thought bitterly, as he poured dipper after dipper of cold water over his head. It burned where the cane had cut his skin. He scrubbed his face, his body and legs right down to the toes until he felt he was clean. When he came out of the bathroom with the towel around his waist, his mother called him. He went and stood before her. She looked at him up and down, and nodded. He thought she looked sad.

In the bedroom, he looked at his face in the little mirror hanging from the window frame. His eyes were still red. There was no trace of mud on his face. He felt better. He thought how nice it would have been if he had swum in a proper swimming pool like Lim. He thought of Lim in Singapore, swimming in the biggest swimming pool in the world, with a lifeguard watching over him.

* * *

Two days later. It had rained heavily that night. It was cool until the afternoon. Then the heat picked up. He couldn't help thinking about the cool waters of the pit. There was no pain or marks on the back of his legs. It felt like he had not actually been caned. After lunch, he lay down in the front room, looking at an old Kid Carson comic book. He was halfway through the book when he heard the sound, "*Swin, swin.*"

---

8 Father in Tamil.

Author's Note

I began writing the story with just the idea of the boys swimming in the pit. I wrote it in three days and put it away. After a few days, I went back. I read through it and made the necessary changes. After a few more days, I went through it again and it was done. Sometimes, I go through a story more than ten times, tinkering with it. It may not be the same with other writers. It may not work for all writers.

Sometimes, I allow the story to write itself, meaning to say, I allow stray thoughts to come in as I write. I decide later whether they fit in and are helpful in driving the narrative. If not, I remove them.

When Hemingway was asked how to write, he just said, "Write. Write the truest sentence you can."

To me, it means one should write about what one knows. Each sentence must be necessary to tell the story. The sentences should help to build the picture and drive the story to its end.

Dialogue, if handled well, can show what is happening and how the characters are feeling, driving the story along.

Each writer has to find his voice, his style and how he writes best. Different kinds of stories need different ways of telling. For a beginner, one should just start by writing about anything. Just pick an idea and write whatever comes to mind, without worrying where or how it is going to end. It is only writing. It can be changed and rewritten until one is satisfied, and one should write to the best of his or her ability.

About the Writers

Raymund P Reyes was born and raised in Tacloban City in the eastern part of the Philippines, and currently lives in Ottawa. He has taught English as Second Language in the Philippines, Saudi Arabia and Canada. His works have been published in various literary journals and anthologies, such as *Your Impossible Voice, Carbon Culture Review, New Reader Magazine, Philippine Speculative Fiction X, On the Back of a Motorbike: Stories and Poems from Southeast Asia* and *Verses Typhoon Yolanda: A Storm of Filipino Poets.*

Babitha Marina Justin is an associate professor in English, a poet and an artist. A Pushcart Prize nominee 2018, her poems and short stories have appeared in many journals like *Eclectica, Esthetic Apostle, The Paragon Press, Fulcrum, The Scriblerus, Trampset, Constellations*, etc. She has published two collections of poems, *Of Fireflies, Guns and the Hills* (2015) and *I Cook My Own Feast* (2019). She will debut as a novelist with *Natal Tooth* (2021).

Sachiko Kashiwaba is a prolific writer of children's and young adult fantasy whose career spans more than four decades. Her works have garnered the prestigious Sankei, Shogakukan, and Noma children's literature awards, and her novel *The Mysterious Village Veiled in Mist* influenced Hayao Miyazaki's film *Spirited Away.* Her books for children include the Monster Hotel series, *Great-Aunt's Amazing Recipes, Miracle Family, The What's-Next Library, Temple Alley Summer, The Witch Who Loved the King* and *Strange Journey from the Basement*, lately animated as *The Wonderland.* She edited a children's version of the *Tōno monogatari*, beloved folk legends collected by Kizen Sasaki and Kunio Yanagita. She lives in Iwate Prefecture, Japan.

Avery Fischer Udagawa (Translator)
Avery Fischer Udagawa's translations from Japanese to English include *J-Boys: Kazuo's World, Tokyo, 1965* by Shogo Oketani, "Festival Time" by Ippei Mogami in *The Best Asian Short Stories 2018* and *Temple Alley Summer* by Sachiko Kashiwaba. Her translations have also appeared in *Kyoto Journal* and *Words Without Borders*. She lives near Bangkok, Thailand.

Niduparas Erlang was born in Serang in 1986. He writes stories, novels, essays and articles in journalism. His latest novel, *Burung Kayu (Wooden Bird*, 2020), received special jury recognition in the 2019 Jakarta Arts Council Novel Competition and won the prestigious Khatulistiwa Literary Award in 2020. His other books include the short story collections *La Rangku (The Kite Prince*, 2011, winner of the 2011 Surabaya Arts Festival Short Story Manuscript Competition), *Penanggung Tiga Butir Lada Hitam di Dalam Pusar (The One with Three Peppercorns in His Bellybutton*, 2015, winner of the 2015 Siwa Nataraja Short Story Manuscript Award) and a 2017 volume which includes both collections. He currently runs the Aing Community, facilitates the interdisciplinary cultural heritage and arts center Banten Girang Laboratorium, and helps to manage the Multatuli Art Festival. He received his Masters in Cultural Studies with an Oral Traditions specialisation from Indonesia University and is an Indonesian literature professor at Pamulang University.

Annie Tucker (Translator)
Annie Tucker is an Los Angeles-based writer, researcher and translator from Indonesia. She holds a PhD in Culture and Performance from University of California, Los Angeles. Her translation of Eka Kurniawan's *Beauty is a Wound* was a *New York Times* notable book and won the 2016 World Reader's Award.

Janani Janarthanan is a blogger of four years and a budding short story writer. She holds a triple major degree in English Literature, Mass Communication and Psychology. She has previously published a short story and an article on period poverty during the pandemic at Women's Web and Menstrupedia.com, respectively. As an aspiring culture journalist, she is passionate about stories of arts and culture, and writes on contemporary topics with a strong, autobiographical touch. She can be found online at www.yarnsofideas.wordpress.in.

Asma' Jailani is a content writer who plans to further her studies in Creative Writing and English Literature at the University of East Anglia in the United Kingdom. In 2016 and 2017, she won first place in the Asian English Olympics Short Story Writing division. She lives in Malaysia, where she is content to dream up more stories and the possibility of publishing her own novel in the future.

Clara Mok graduated from Nanyang Technological University, Singapore. She was selected for the Mentor Access Project 2016/17 by the National Arts Council in Singapore. "The Many Painted Faces of Chinese Opera" was developed under Josephine Chia's mentorship. Her short stories are published in *Writing the City*

– Fresh Fiction from Singapore and in online literary publications. She is an English educator and shares her love for writing with her students. She loves reminiscing about her childhood and wishes to capture snippets of Singapore's past before they disappear.

Maureen SY Tai is an emerging writer and artist who aspires to write for children. After spending most of her childhood and youth in Malaysia, she has lived and/or worked as a lawyer/corporate financier in Japan, Canada, the United Kingdom, and her current home, Hong Kong. Maureen's creative works have been published by *Cha: An Asian Literary Journal*, the Asian American Writers' Workshop and Oxford University Press. She has also contributed to literary anthologies in Hong Kong (*Imprint 19*) and Singapore (*Unmasked: Reflections on Virus-time*), to online magazines and has been shortlisted in children's writing competitions. Proudly and unabashedly Malaysian, Maureen speaks and dreams in five languages. Together with her two children, she writes children's book reviews on her family blog, www.storiesthatstaywithus.com.

Tripat Narayanan, writer and film/theatre critic, has written for Malaysian and Indian publications, such as *The New Straits Times, The Edge, The Sun, Malaysian Tatler, Men's Review, Her World* and *Angarag*. She has judged the theatre category of the Boh Cameronian Arts Awards. She has also served on film panels in Hyderabad and Penang, and was invited as a guest to the Cannes Film Festival. Her coffee table book, *Table: Food, Frangipanis and Flair*, won two Gourmand International Awards: Best Innovative Food book and Best First Food book in 2005. Tripat was educated at the University of Malaya (English Literature and Cinema Studies) and was awarded a Fulbright scholarship in 1976 to attend Northwestern University, Illinois, to pursue a doctorate in Film Studies. She received a second Fulbright award for a Teaching Fellowship at Emmanuel College, Boston. She lives in Kuala Lumpur where she continues to muse on words.

Charlotte Hammond is based in New York City and works in the fashion industry as a copywriter. She is an active member of the Jersey City Writers, a rich community of authors and poets. Her fiction works have appeared in *Pithead Chapel*, *The Basil O'Flaherty* and others. She lived and worked as a writer in Seoul, South Korea, from 2013 to 2016. She won first place in the Literature Translation Institute of Korea's Essay Contest in 2014.

Muthusamy Pon Ramiah was writing articles for a trade union quarterly newsletter for about 15 years before writing fiction. His novel was longlisted for the 2021 Epigram Books Fiction Prize. Ramiah has published two short stories, "This Thing About Rings" and "Red Eyes" in *Anak Sastra*, an online magazine. His story about the COVID-19 experience, "Ini Musim Coronavirus" (This is the Coronavirus Season) was included in the book, *Unmasked: Reflections on Virus-time* and another short story "City Dwellers" in *KL Noir: Magic* (2021).

About the Editor

Anitha Devi Pillai (PhD) has authored and edited creative and non-creative fiction books as well as translated a historical fiction novel, *Sembawang: A Novel* (2020) from Tamil into English. She also loves writing poetry, some of which have made their way into the classrooms in Singapore, India, Australia, and the Philippines. Many of her works explore themes such as identity, heritage, and culture.

She is best known for her research into the Singapore Malayalee community that was supported by a National Heritage Board (Singapore) grant and resulted in the publication of *From Kerala to Singapore: Voices from the Singapore Malayalee Community* (2017) For this study, Anitha was awarded a 'Pravasi Express Research Excellence Award' in 2017.

Her other books are *Project Work: Exploring Processes, Practices and Strategies* (2008), *From Estate to Embassy: Memories of an Ambassador* (2019), A *View of Stars: Stories of Love* (2020), and *The Story of Onam* (in press).

Anitha's favourite genres to write are the short story and creative non-fiction prose. Her stories have appeared in various anthologies including *The Best Asian Short Stories 2019*, *Letter to my Son* (2020) and *Food Republic: A Singapore Literary Banquet* (2020). She is currently writing a collection of short stories focusing on food and love.

In a parallel life, she is an applied linguist and teacher educator at the National Institute of Education (NIE), Nanyang Technological University (NTU), Singapore where she teaches courses on various forms of writing and trains English language teachers to teach writing. Anitha is a three-time recipient of teaching awards: 'Excellence in Teaching Commendation Award' from NIE, NTU in 2018 and the 'SUSS Teaching Merit Award' in 2014 and 2013 from the Singapore University of Social Sciences.